Going the Distance

Also by Mary Jane Miller

Me and My Name

Upside Down

Fast Forward

Going the Distance

MARY JANE MILLER

VIKING

For my daughters,
Karen, Colleen, Melinda, and Leanne,
with all my love.

VIKING
Published by the Penguin Group
Penguin Books USA Inc., 375 Hudson Street, New York, New York 10014, U.S.A.
Penguin Books Ltd, 27 Wrights Lane, London W8 5TZ, England
Penguin Books Australia Ltd, Ringwood, Victoria, Australia
Penguin Books Canada Ltd, 10 Alcorn Avenue, Toronto, Ontario, Canada M4V 3B2
Penguin Books (N.Z.) Ltd, 182–190 Wairau Road, Auckland 10, New Zealand

Penguin Books Ltd, Registered Offices: Harmondsworth, Middlesex, England

First published in 1994 by Viking, a division of Penguin Books USA Inc.

1 3 5 7 9 10 8 6 4 2

LIBRARY OF CONGRESS CATALOGING-IN-PUBLICATION DATA
Miller, Mary Jane.
Going the distance / Mary Jane Miller.   p.   cm.
Summary: Loren wants to stay in one place, make friends, and be on
a swimming team, but her parents are artists who keep moving every
few months.
ISBN 0-670-84815-8
[1. Artists—Fiction.   2. Swimming—Fiction.   3. Household,
Moving—Fiction.   4. Hair—Fiction.]   I. Title.
PZ7.M6312Go 1994 [Fic]—dc20 94-20289 CIP AC

Printed in the U.S.A.
Set in Palatino

· acknowledgments ·

I give my thanks to my editor, Deborah Brodie, who steers me through the shoals and challenges of writing with loving encouragement, wisdom, and unfailing good humor; to my agent, Jane Jordan Browne, for her many kindnesses; to my niece Jennifer Miller who generously and patiently answered all my questions. For significant details, I would like to thank Elizabeth Aamodt, Mary Jane Biskupic, Rob and Rebecca Chambers, Mary Ewing, Dorothy Knudson, Cecelia Miller, Joseph Miller, Joan Nelson, and Lois Osborn. A very special thanks to Denise Zielinski, Marlene Stratton, Lynn Reeder, Teddy Martinson, Mary Marshall, Joanne Lize, Sue Eilers, and Jeannie Arinyanontakoon of the Helen Plum Library, and Sharon Ball of the Villa Park Library. I am forever grateful to Leanne and Melinda, who patiently read with insight and good cheer. To Karen, Tom, and David Boston; Colleen, Don, Katie, and Sara Reid a loving thank you. And as always, I am most grateful to Joe who goes the distance with me. Thank you, Maude. And thank you, Thaddeus and company.

Going the Distance

· chapter one ·

Mom and I were sitting on the beach. As usual, Mom had her sketchbook, pencils, and props with her. She brushed my hair until she decided it was perfect, then she threw a striped poncho over my head and handed me a seashell.

When I wrinkled up my nose and rolled my eyes, Mom laughed. She said, "No funny faces allowed," and began to sketch.

I sat very still, eyes centered on the horizon, and thought about Stephanie, my best friend. I wished we were swimming in and out of the waves, moving closer and closer to the breakers.

The longer I sat, the hotter and heavier the poncho grew. "Mom," I complained, "I'm going into meltdown."

"Just one more minute," Mom said. She looked at me, but didn't see me.

Blowing your breath on your face does not cool you off. Neither does rolling your shoulders around.

"Please sit still," Mom said.

I sat as still as I could for as long as I could. I know what eternity feels like. My head and back started to itch. The no-see-ums were probably eating me alive. Sweat dripped off my nose. It was disgusting. I couldn't stand it. I threw the poncho down on the sand and announced, "I'm going swimming."

Mom continued to sketch. When she finally looked, really looked, at me, I stuck my tongue out as far as it would go and panted like a puppy.

"Poor baby," Mom said. She laughed, and then she said, "You and your swimming. You're just like your grandfather, part fish."

I really don't know my grandfather; he lives in Italy. I didn't say anything. Mom said, "Come here and I'll braid your hair."

My hair hangs below my waist, so I said okay. While Mom was doing my braids, we saw Dad running up the beach toward us. He was waving something small and white.

When he reached Mom and me, he didn't smile, he didn't say anything, he just handed Mom a letter. Her eyes grew big and her hands shook as she held it to her lips. "I'm afraid to open it," she whispered.

What could be in a letter that would make Mom shake? "Who's it from?" I asked.

"Rimini," Mom answered in a quivery voice.

I looked at Dad. "Why is it a big deal?" Mom gets a letter from my grandfather every two weeks.

Dad shook his head and put his finger to his lips. Mom took a deep breath, opened the envelope, and took out two letters. While she was reading, she gave a little gasp. Then she walked to the edge of the water and stood still.

"Is it bad news, Dad?" I asked.

Before he could answer my question, Mom came running back to us. "The galleries have accepted one of my paintings!" she shouted, waving her arms and the letters.

Dad grinned. "Yes! Yes! Yes! I *knew* it would happen." He put his arms around Mom and danced with her, right there on the beach. Then they hugged and kissed. It was very embarrassing.

"You guys, will someone please tell me what's going on?"

Mom and Dad stopped kissing. "Your grandfather's paintings are going on exhibit in Rome, Paris, and London," Mom said. "And the galleries are going to show one of *my* paintings with his." Mom's eyes sparkled and danced. She put her arm across my shoulder and pulled me close. "It's because of you, Loren."

"What did I have to do with it?"

"Everything. *Loren in the Garden* is the chosen painting."

I backed away. "I look worse than dorky in that picture." Mom made me wear an old-fashioned, long white dress, sit on the grass, and stare at the red rose I was holding in my hand.

"Loren," Dad said. He put his arms across my shoulders. "You could never look dorky. You have to remember your mother's painting is a work of art and so are you."

"Dad! You need new glasses." A short, skinny almost twelve-year-old kid with bushy eyebrows, dark brown eyes, and hair the color of sand isn't a work of art—unless it's for the cover of a comic book.

"Loren, no arguments. No pouting. Come on, race you to the van."

"But I was going swimming."

"Later," Dad said.

While we were driving home, Mom read the letter from Rimini out loud. I didn't pay any attention until Mom read the part that said, "You must come for the gallery showings. I am there only because of you and Andrew. How proud I will be to have you by my side."

"Mom! Are you *really* going to Europe, again?"

When Mom turned around to look at me, a soft smile played around her lips. She sighed. "It's a dream come true, Loren. I have to go."

"How long will you be gone?"

Mom nodded. "At least three months. Maybe even a little longer."

Longer? What's with Mom and Dad? Mom was acting as if she didn't care that she'd be far away from Dad and me. Dad was acting strange, too. Why wasn't he mad, or sad?

Then whoosh, it hit me like a ten-ton wave. I knew why Mom and Dad were acting so cool. "I have to go with you, don't I? What about school?"

Silence. I held my breath, hoping Mom and Dad would say, You're wrong, you don't have to leave—but they didn't. After I gulped down the lump that was stuck in my throat I managed to say, "I thought we were going to stay in Florida. That we wouldn't move for a long time. Maybe never."

Mom turned around and reached out her hand to me. "I'm sorry, Loren," she said softly. "I didn't know we'd be leaving here . . . so soon."

"I don't believe you!" I yelled. "You and Dad must have talked about it. You didn't decide just *now*, on the beach, to move . . . to Europe."

"We're not moving to Europe," Dad said.

"We're just going for a few months," Mom added. "And yes, we did talk about it."

"You didn't talk to me. I don't want to go to Europe, I have to go to school. And I want to be on the swimming team with Stephanie."

"Loren, you're not going to Europe," Dad said. "We'd take you, but you're right, you have to go to school. So while we're gone, you'll be with Nelia."

"But Dad, I don't—"

Dad went right on talking just as if I hadn't

tried to say something. "You know your grand-mother will be delighted to have you for a visit."

"But we're going to do that anyway. You promised we'd visit Nelia this year at Christmas-time." Before Dad or Mom could say anything, I said, "Why don't you understand, I don't want to leave Hemingway and go to another school, even for a little while. Dad, why can't *you* stay here with me?"

Dad didn't answer me. "Mom, why can't Dad stay?"

"Loren, your dad and I won't be gone that long."

"That's what you said before, the last time you went to visit Rimini. And you were gone for a whole year."

"This time, it's different," Mom said.

She put her head back against the seat, Dad turned on the radio, and I stared out the window and counted up the months I had gone to school in Los Olas. It added up to four.

I had started sixth grade in North Carolina, but in March we moved here, to Florida. School was over in June. That's four months.

Last year, in fifth grade, we lived in California and New Mexico. The year before that we were in

New York—that's where we used to live before Mom and Dad went to Europe. When they came back, someone else was living in our apartment.

Mom and Dad didn't care. They wanted to live where it was sunny and warm anyway.

I hate having to move. I hate *always* being the new kid. I looked down at my hands. They had turned into fists.

I locked my fingers together as Dad whipped the van around the corner and drove into a mini-mall. "Be right back," he said. Mom and I watched him run into a florist shop.

Two minutes later, Dad was back with a bouquet of balloons. He gave Mom two "Congratulations" and three "I Love You" balloons. He handed me a red-and-white "Let's Kiss and Make Up" balloon, then he reached in and planted a quick kiss on my forehead. Mom leaned over and blew me two kisses.

Just like that, they thought the fight was over. It may be over for them, but not for me, I thought. I let my balloon sit on the floor.

The rest of the way home, Mom and Dad sang, mostly songs Dad had written. My head started to ache when they sang "Where I Once Belonged" for the seventh time. Then they sang old songs

like "Me and My Gal" and "On the Road Again."
Those songs didn't make me feel any better.

I closed my eyes and pretended I was swimming in the ocean, diving in and out of the waves.
I must have fallen asleep; before I knew it, we were pulling up to our condo.

I didn't say one word in the elevator, but while Mom was arranging her balloons, I asked Dad, "Why won't you stay with me?"

Dad sighed. He brushed his hair behind his ears and pulled me into the kitchen. "I can't," he whispered.

"Why not?"

"When you're grown up, you'll understand," Dad said.

Why do parents blow you off like that? "I want to know now, Dad."

Dad pushed his glasses up on top of his head. "It's not that we want to leave you, Loren. But we have to be with Rimini. We have to see his paintings and your mother's portrait of you on exhibit. It's a very special time for us."

"But Dad, what about me?" I started to ask.

"Loren," Dad said, interrupting, "listen to me. This trip is very important to your mother. You don't want to make her unhappy, do you?"

What kind of a question is that? A question with only one answer. "No."

"And don't you miss your grandmother?"

"Yes, but—"

"No buts." Dad put his hand on my shoulder.

"But Dad"—I had to make him understand—"school starts next week. Why can't I stay here? Mrs. Rodriguez is right next door."

Dad shook his head and laughed. "Loren, we're not doing *Home Alone 3*."

"Dad! I wasn't asking a dumb kid question. Maybe Mrs. Rodriguez would let me live with her. Or I could stay with Stephanie until you get back. Her mom says I'm always welcome."

"And I'm sure she means it, but the answer is no, Loren."

"But Dad, you let me stay with Nelia for a whole year when you and Mom went to Europe the last time."

Dad shook his head. "That was different and this time we'll only be gone a few months."

"Hey, you two, what's the big secret?" Mom asked, as she walked into the kitchen.

"Big plans here," Dad said, "for a celebration dinner."

"Sounds good to me," Mom said. She smiled

10

and stroked my cheek with her finger. "Nelia won't believe how much you've grown. I can hardly believe it myself."

A couple of inches is no big deal. I'm one of the shortest kids at Hemingway.

That night dinner was a big deal. Dad fixed shrimp scampi, Mom stuffed artichokes, I made the salad and lit the candles. When we finished, Mom asked Dad, "Shall we call Nelia?"

Dad nodded. "Loren, do you want to tell Nelia our news?"

I shook my head.

Dad dialed Nelia's number. He told her all about Europe and Rimini, then he asked her about me.

Say no, Nelia. Say no. If she did, then Mom and Dad would have to let me stay with Mrs. Rodriguez or Stephanie. But when Dad gave Mom the thumbs-up sign, I knew Nelia had said yes.

After Mom talked to Nelia, she handed me the receiver. "I'm so happy you're coming back for a long visit, Loren," Nelia said, "but I know that changing schools again has to be really hard for you."

"Big time," I said. "I've got to go now."

"Loren, you know you can call me whenever you want to talk."

"I know," I said. After I hung up, I turned on the TV and stared at a rerun of *Life Goes On*. When Mom and Dad came back into the living room, I looked up and asked, "When are we leaving?"

"As soon as possible," Mom said.

"When's that?"

"By the end of the week," Dad answered.

"School starts next week. Where am I going to go?"

"Where I went," Dad answered. "Lake Shore Junior High. You'll like it."

"No I won't," I muttered as I left the room. I slammed my bedroom door as hard as I could.

I tried calling Stephanie, but when her answering machine answered with, "You have reached the Turners . . . " I hung up.

You can lie on your back and stare at the ceiling for about fifteen minutes before you get a crick in your neck. I turned over, but who could sleep?

One of the thousand and two good things about living in Florida is having your own balcony. The air was almost too heavy to breathe, but I didn't care. Mrs. Rodriguez was swimming laps in the pool. I leaned over the railing and watched her go back and forth, back and forth.

When the pool lights went out, I went back inside, opened my bottom dresser drawer, and took out all the pictures of Stephanie and me. I stuck them under my pillow, except for the picture Steph's dad took of us at the beach. I fell asleep holding on to that one.

·chapter two·

The next morning, I called Nelia back. When I told her that Dad said I was going to his old school, Lake Shore Junior High, Nelia said, "Don't worry, I'll get all the forms. By the time you're here, everything will be worked out so you can start right away."

"Thanks, Nelia." Now I wouldn't have to sit in the school office and fill out a million papers.

Nelia and I talked some more about school. Just before we hung up, she said, "Oh. I almost forgot to tell you. Twins moved in next door. A boy and a girl."

"How old are they?" I asked.

14

"Around your age, I think. Maybe you can walk to school with them?"

Nelia couldn't be serious. Kids, especially guys, don't want to hang around with people they don't know.

After Nelia and I said good-bye, I called Stephanie. No one answered. I left a message on the machine: "Call me ASAP. Or sooner."

Stephanie finally called me, right before dinner. "Didn't you get my message? Where have you been?" I growled.

"We stayed at my cousins' last night. And today I went shopping for school clothes with my mom. Why?"

"Because . . . because I have something to tell you." I took a king-sized breath and said, "I'm not going to Hemingway with you."

"What! Why?" Stephanie shrieked.

"My parents are going to Italy, and I'm going to stay with my grandmother while they're gone."

"You just got here."

"I know."

"Does your grandmother live in Florida?"

"No. She lives in Lake Shore."

"Where's that?"

"It's near Chicago."

"Chicago!" Stephanie yelled. "Are you serious? You might as well be going to Alaska or the North Pole. Are you going to be there forever?"

"I don't think so. Mom and Dad keep saying it's a visit. I'm hoping we'll be back here in January."

"January. That's next year. What about the swimming team?"

"Tell them about me. Then I can sign up when I get back."

The day before we left, Stephanie invited me to her house for dinner. Stephanie lives near the ocean, so we swam, sunned, and looked for shells most of the afternoon.

Before we went back to Stephanie's house, we snapped a whole roll of pictures. Toward the end of the roll, we got silly. Stephanie put her glasses on her head and pulled her long black braid over her mouth. "The mustache look is very in," she said as I took her picture.

I stood on my head and said, "Things are looking up," while Stephanie took my picture. She took another one as I fell over.

A lady walking her dog stopped and said she'd take a picture of us together. We both blinked when she snapped.

When it was time to leave, I gulped down the

big hard lump in my throat and said, "See ya."

Stephanie handed me a gift bag. I opened it right away. There were five *First Loves,* including number 196, *None but the Brave,* and hardbound copies of *Jane Eyre* and *Gone with the Wind.*

"Great! Thanks!"

"My mom says they are *the* most romantic novels," Stephanie said.

Steph and I love to read, especially romance.

"Promise me you'll write," I said as I walked out the door. She promised.

"BFF," Stephanie whispered as we walked down the driveway.

"Best friends forever," I said and I hugged Steph good-bye.

As Dad pulled the van out of the driveway, I shouted out the window, "I'll call you when I get to my grandmother's! And don't forget to send me the pictures."

Early the next morning, we were ready to leave. It never takes us long to pack up; that's because we always rent a condo or house that has furniture. Mom and Dad think it's best to travel light, which is why we left our stuff in our New York apartment. The only furniture we have with us is my dollhouse furniture.

While we were fitting the boxes and suitcases into the van, Dad sang "Rolling, Rolling." He does that every time we move.

Right before we pulled out onto the road, I remembered I had left my rock and seashell collections on the kitchen table. The books from Stephanie were there, too. "Wait! We can't go yet!" I yelled.

Dad stopped the van. "Why? What's wrong?"

"I forgot my seashells, rocks, and books."

Dad shook his head. "I locked the door. You'll have to get the key from Mrs. Rodriguez."

"Don't take forever," Mom added. "We want to get started."

Mrs. Rodriguez was in her kitchen eating an orange and reading the paper. She smiled at me. "Pull up a chair, sit down. Have an orange."

"Thanks, but Mom and Dad are waiting for me." I told Mrs. Rodriguez about my seashells. "I need the key to get in."

When I unlocked the door and walked into our old apartment, the rooms looked the same, but it wasn't home anymore. Except for my things on the kitchen table, everything that said *The Monroes live here* was gone.

That's why each time we move, I hide something somewhere. There's a rock behind the TV in New Mexico, a sketch I made of my dollhouse under my bed in San Francisco, and my third-grade picture is in my bottom drawer at Nelia's house.

It didn't take me long to hide a black-and-white striped shell under the sofa. I wondered if anyone would ever find it.

When I got back to Mrs. Rodriguez's apartment, she gave me an orange, and a big hug. She said, "It's been nice knowing you, little one." She pointed her finger at me. "I will miss you."

"I'll miss you, too," I said. I thanked her, gave her a quick kiss, and ran out to the van. Dad was beeping the horn.

Stephanie was right. It's a long way to Chicago. I read two of Nelia's mysteries—she writes them—started *Jane Eyre*, listened to my Walkman, won two and lost three games of solitaire, wrote a letter to Stephanie, and kept my mouth shut. Mom and Dad gave up trying to get me to talk.

We stayed overnight at a motel in Kentucky. When I got into bed, I closed my eyes and wished I was back at Los Olas. Stephanie and I would be on the beach, looking for shells, diving in and out of the waves, catching some rays, talking about school.

It was pouring rain when we left the next morning. It was too dark to read, so I plugged myself into my Walkman and listened to the Seals' new album, *Rippling Waters.*

I must have fallen asleep, because when I opened my eyes, the sun was shining. Mom was driving and Dad was making soft little snoring sounds. "Are we almost to Nelia's?" I whispered.

"Almost but not quite. We've just left Indiana. We're in Illinois."

Two hours later, we pulled up to Nelia's house. Everything looked the same. The two giant oak trees still guarded the front door, pots of bright pink geraniums were on the porch, and when I tilted my head back, I could see my tower room.

Nelia must have heard us, because she opened the front door before I could ring the bell. "Loren, is it really you?" she asked.

Before I could answer, I was in Nelia's arms. We hugged for a long time, then we walked down to the van together.

Dad said, "Hi Mom," and put his arm around her shoulders. Mom gave Nelia a quick little kiss on the cheek.

Nelia picked up one of the suitcases, and we followed her into the house. Nelia said, "I've changed things around a little bit." She hesitated. "Since . . . since you've been gone." She headed for the curvy wooden staircase. The tenth step still creaked.

I ran my hand along the banister. "Hey, Nelia," I said, "remember the day I slid down the banister?"

"I remember," Mom said. "You landed in the hospital."

"How do you remember?" I asked. "You were in Europe."

"When we came home, you showed me right where you fell."

"I really scared Nelia that day."

"Seeing blood does that to me," Nelia said. "It's easier to write about it. But Loren and I both survived the day, didn't we?"

I nodded. Mom didn't say anything and neither did Dad.

When we reached the top of the stairs, a fluffy white cat with one blue and one orange eye stared at us. "Agatha!" I yelled. I scooped her up and put my face close to hers. "You are so pretty."

"It's hard to believe," Dad said, "that my mother, Cornelia Monroe, has a cat in her house."

Nelia laughed and said, "You know, Andrew, things and people have a way of changing."

"I forget," Mom said, "when did you get Agatha?"

I answered for Nelia. "Right after we left, Nelia found her at the Humane Society. She wrote me all about it. I told you. Remember?"

Dad grinned. "The Agatha Christie cat." He turned to Mom. "Remember, you said, what else would a mystery writer name her cat?"

Nelia shook her head. "Never mind. Writers are allowed their eccentricities."

We all followed Nelia down the long hall. When she opened one of the bedroom doors, she said to Mom and Dad, "I redecorated your—I mean this room last year. I thought white walls would brighten it up a bit."

"Fine. Great," Dad said.

"We appreciate you . . . taking care of Loren . . . for us . . . while we're away, Nelia," Mom said.

Nelia smiled and nodded, but she didn't say anything. Nobody did. It was as if we were all on pause.

"Can I see my old room now?" I asked.

Nelia and I climbed the short flight of stairs to the tower room. "The pink wallpaper is gone," I said out loud. The walls were blue. "But my bed is still here." I ran my hand over the blue-and-white polka-dot comforter. "And I can put my dollhouse back in the same corner."

Nelia smiled. "I guess that means you like it?"

I nodded. "You remembered that blue is my favorite color now."

"Yes, but, this is *your* room, so you can change whatever you want."

"Does that mean I can put up my pictures? We could never put anything on the walls in our condos."

"You can put up whatever you want, except," Nelia raised one eyebrow, "I still draw the line at Ninja Turtles."

I laughed. It's hard to believe now, but in third grade, I was in love with Michelangelo. "You don't have to worry," I said. "I have pictures and posters of dolphins, whales, and Olympic swimmers now."

While we were talking, Dad came into the room. "Three kids are on the porch. They're looking for you, Loren," he said.

"For me? I don't know anybody."

•chapter three•

The front door was open when I came downstairs. Two guys and a girl were standing on the front steps. "Hi, I'm Ellie," the girl said. "Are you Loren?"

"Dumb question. Who else would she be?" the guy with the long reddish-brown hair said.

Ellie rolled her eyes. "You're such a dork, RJ. Ignore my brother."

"You're the twins," I said.

RJ clapped his hands over his head.

"Not nice, RJ." Ellie gave his arm a punch.

RJ doubled over, groaned, and grabbed his arm. "Watch it, Nolan, Spiderwoman is on the loose."

The skinny guy with blond bangs and a sunburned nose jumped off the porch. RJ followed him.

Ellie shook her head. "Sometimes guys are just *too* weird." She handed me a piece of paper. "This is for you."

"What is it?" I asked.

"The bus schedule for school. Your grandmother asked me to get one for you."

"Are you going to ride the bus?" I asked.

Ellie shook her head. "No, we're going to ride our bikes. See ya at school, Monday."

"See ya," I called after Ellie, as she ran down the stairs.

At least now I know three people by name, I told myself. I found Mom, Dad, and Nelia in the kitchen drinking root beer.

"Who were you talking to?" Mom asked.

"The kids next door. Ellie and RJ and their friend, Nolan."

"Did Ellie bring you the bus schedule?" Nelia asked.

I nodded and put the schedule on the table. "Where's Agatha?" I asked.

"Oh, she's off hiding somewhere," Nelia replied, "probably under the table in the garden room."

"Is that the room you wrote me about, the one that took forever to finish?" I asked.

Nelia nodded. "That's the one."

"Wait until you see it, Loren. It has a wall of windows." Mom grabbed my hand. "Come on, I'll show you."

Mom walked around the garden room as if she were a tour guide. She went on and on about how it was the perfect room for painting. "Your grandfather would love this room."

When I didn't say anything, Mom said, "Hello, you're not with me." I shrugged. Mom persisted. "Come on, tell me what's going on in that head of yours."

"I have to ride the bus Monday. By myself."

"Why is that a problem?" Mom didn't let me answer her question. She said, "You'll make friends, Loren. You always do. You've already met—what are their names?"

"Ellie, RJ, and Nolan. But they're not taking the bus."

"Why is that a problem?"

"Mom, I don't know what the kids on the bus are like."

"I'm sure they're nice kids."

"You don't know that, Mom. This is junior high and junior high is different."

"No, it's not," Mom insisted. She shook her head. "Loren, you say the same thing about every school."

"That's because every school is different. You never had to change schools, so you don't know."

Mom laughed and shook her head. "That's not so. I went to two schools, Saint Mary's, just like you did, and then Claremont."

"Two is nothing, Mom. Lake Shore will be my seventh school."

"Seven!" Mom said "seven" as if the number was a big surprise. She shook her head. "I know it's hard for you to be changing schools all the time."

I shrugged and said, "I liked Hemingway."

"And I'm sure you'll like Lake Shore. I know your dad did."

"Mom, that was a long time ago." Why do parents think you're just like them? They're old.

Later on, while I was unpacking, Nelia knocked on my door and asked if I needed any help. I said, sure.

While I was putting my socks and underwear

away, I looked in the bottom drawer of the dresser for my third-grade picture. It was gone. I must have had a puzzled look on my face because Nelia asked, "What's wrong?"

"I can't find my picture."

"Follow me," Nelia said. We went into her bedroom. On the dresser in a pretty silver frame was my third-grade picture.

Looking at yourself in an old picture is almost like looking at a stranger. "I look different," I said. "My hair is a lot longer now."

After I put the picture back on Nelia's dresser, I asked her when she found it. "Right after you left," Nelia said, "when I was putting some of my summer clothes in your drawer. It was an unexpected present."

"Oh, I almost forgot," I said. "I brought you a present." I took Nelia by the hand and pulled her back to the tower.

My rock jar was sitting on the windowsill. I dug down until I found the black-and-purple rock. "It's really cool. I'll show you." I held the rock in the palm of my hand. "See how the colors change when you hold it to the light."

Nelia nodded. "It's beautiful." She smiled and said, "Thank you. I'll put it on my desk and every day I'll watch the changing colors and think of you."

After dinner, Mom and Dad said I could call Stephanie, if Nelia didn't mind. She didn't.

I used the calling card Mom and Dad had given me. Mom set the timer for fifteen minutes. Stephanie shrieked when she heard my voice. The first thing I did was give her Nelia's telephone number. "Promise you'll call," I said.

Stephanie promised and then we talked about school. "Just think, you won't have Demon Dreiser for math," she said. "I bet even Arnold Schwarzenegger would be afraid of her."

I had to agree that escaping from Dreiser was the one good thing about Lake Shore.

Stephanie said the one good thing about Hemingway was her mother was going to let her wear makeup to school. "What about you?" she asked.

I laughed. "My mom let me wear makeup? Oh sure! On the same day she lets me cut my hair."

Bong! The timer went off. "Steph, I've got to go."

"Wait. Wait. Did you meet anyone?" I told Stephanie about Ellie, RJ, and Nolan. "Lucky you! Two guys! Are they gorgeous?"

"No."

"Are they cute?"

"Sort of, I guess."

"Which one is the cutest?"

"RJ. I've got to go, Steph. Call me."

"I'll call you next week for sure," she promised.

That night I couldn't sleep. The first few nights in a new place, I'm always wide awake. It takes a while to get used to the sounds.

Agatha pushed my door open, jumped up on the bed, and stretched out on my pillow. She purred when I stroked her back, and that was a nice sound. "Pretty girl," I said. Agatha licked my ear as if to say thank you.

The next morning, while Nelia and I were having breakfast, she put down her coffee cup and placed her hand over mine. "Two quarters for your thoughts."

I shrugged. "I was thinking about Monday. I wish I didn't have to go to school on the bus."

Nelia frowned. "Why?" she asked.

"When you're the new kid, you don't know where to sit. If you sit in the wrong seat, like I did in New Mexico, you can get caught in the middle of a Super-Soaker war."

"It sounds dangerous," Nelia said.

I nodded. "It is. My hair didn't dry until recess, and soggy peanut butter and jelly is the worst sandwich in the world. So now"—I blew out a sigh that moved the napkin—"I sit right behind the driver, even if it is the dork seat."

Nelia shook her head. "This time you won't have to go the dork route. You'll be with Ellie, RJ, and Nolan."

"No, I won't. They're riding their bikes."

"Why don't you ride with them?"

"They didn't ask me. And anyway, I don't have a bike."

"What happened to your bike?"

"Somebody stole it right before we left Los Olas, and we didn't have time to get another one."

"You could use my bike. It's in the garage."

"You have a bike? What kind?" I asked cautiously.

The lines around Nelia's eyes crinkle up when she laughs. "Relax, it's not a three-wheeler with a basket," she said. "I know it's hard to imagine your silver-haired grandmother zooming along on a bright red ten-speed but that's what I have. Do you want to see it?"

I nodded and we headed for the garage. The bike was in the corner next to Nelia's car. "It looks like a racer," I said. "I like the white stripes."

"Why don't you go for a ride?"

"My legs aren't long enough." Nelia has long legs. She's almost as tall as my dad, and he's six feet.

"No problem," Nelia said. She adjusted the seat, and I took off. "Don't go too far or stay away too long," Nelia called after me.

Nelia's bike felt as if it was made for me. When I rode past RJ's house, he came zooming down the driveway on his bike. "Cool wheels!" he said when I stopped.

"It's my grandmother's." RJ rolled his eyes. "I'm not lying," I said. "It's true. Honest."

RJ rolled his eyes again, laughed, and said, "My grandmother sky dives."

"Funny." I turned around and rode home. RJ followed me.

As I rode down my driveway, he raced up to the garage and then raced away. "Maybe I'll see you later," he called after me.

"Wait!"

RJ braked. I rode back to him. "Can I ride to school with you guys on Monday?"

·chapter four·

Nelia was in her office writing on her computer. I snuck up behind her, put my hands on her shoulders, and said, "Guess who."

"Oh!" she yelped and put her hand on her chest, then she laughed. "Don't do that to a mystery writer," she said. "We scare easily."

"Sorry. I forgot about knocking," I said.

"Three years is a long time to remember." Nelia waved her hand at the overstuffed chair near her desk. "Sit," she said. "Tell me, how are things going?"

I grinned. "RJ said I could ride to school with them."

"What did your parents say?"

"They said if it was okay with you, it was okay with them."

Later on that afternoon, while Mom and Dad were having lunch in Chicago with old friends of my dad, I went next door to find out what time Ellie, RJ, and Nolan were leaving for school. RJ and Nolan were in the driveway playing serious basketball.

"Hi," I said. No answer. I waited a few minutes and said hi again. Still no answer. I crossed my arms and waited some more. If I were taller, I knew what I'd do. I'd grab the ball and shoot a Michael Jordan basket. They'd notice me for sure if I slam dunked the ball. But being short, I decided the only thing I could do was stand under the hoop and yell, "Is Ellie home?"

"Watch it!" Nolan yelled back as he almost crashed into me.

At least they saw me, I thought, stepping back on the grass.

"Loren! What are you doing here?" Ellie asked. She came down the driveway.

"Looking for you," I replied. "RJ said I could ride with you guys tomorrow."

"He did? I didn't know you had a bike."

After I told Ellie about Nelia's bike, I asked her

34

what time they were leaving for school. "Eight o'clock," she said.

"Guess I'll see you then," I said.

As I was walking back to Nelia's, Ellie called after me, "Wait." I turned around. "Do you want to see my new school clothes?" she asked.

"Yeah, I guess so," I answered.

While we were climbing the stairs to Ellie's room, she asked me what I was going to wear to school. "Jeans, a white shirt, sneakers," I said. "It's what I wear on the first day to every new school. What are you going to wear?"

"My new jeans. But if it's hot, I'm going to wear flowered shorts and a pink top," Ellie said.

Ellie showed me her new clothes and then she said, "I tried to talk my mom into at least one pair of designer jeans, but she leaves the planet if I even whisper *designer*."

"My mom won't buy them either."

Ellie ran her hand over the brown label. "If Lake Shore is a fashion factory, I'm in for major trouble."

"Did you . . . did you go to one of those, too?" I asked.

Ellie nodded. "Last year. I hated it. Most of the kids were label watchers. On the first day at lunch, somebody pulled my collar back to look at the label in my shirt. I didn't know what they were doing."

"That happened to me, too," I told Ellie. "But you know what was funny, at the next school, everybody was doing the grunge look. So I didn't fit in there either."

Ellie nodded. "It's the worst, trying to fit in."

"I know." I folded Ellie's new pink top and said, "We kept on moving so I gave up trying to figure out what everybody was wearing. I like jeans and shirts, and that's what I wear now."

While we were talking, a stone hit the window. Ellie shook her head. "RJ and Nolan are being dorks. Do you want to go down and crash the game?"

Ellie and I went back outside, but the guys were gone, so we sat on the steps and talked. "I wish my hair was long like yours," Ellie said.

"Sometimes it's a major pain," I said. "It takes forever to dry and floats in my face when I go swimming."

"Are you going to get it cut?"

I shook my head. "My mom likes it this way, especially when she paints my picture."

"She paints pictures of you?"

"Tons of them. She's working on one now that she started in Florida."

"Cool," Ellie said.

I shook my head. "Boring!"

Monday morning on our way to school, RJ, Ellie, Nolan and I rode past the bus. It was stopped at the corner. A bunch of kids were piling on. They were laughing and shouting. I could tell everybody knew everybody. Ellie grinned at me when I said, "Boy, am I glad I'm with you guys!"

Lake Shore Junior High had to be ten times the size of Hemingway. We would never have found the office if Nolan hadn't shown us where it was.

After RJ, Ellie, and I handed in all the forms, Ms. Carpenter, the assistant principal, explained how Lake Shore works. "We are a team school," she said. "Each grade level is divided into groups and assigned to a team of teachers for all classes."

Ellie and I gave a little shriek when we discovered we were in the same group. RJ was by himself and so was Nolan.

Near the end of the day, on the way to gym class, Ellie and I agreed that, so far, Lake Shore was okay. No one had checked our labels or blown smoke in our faces in the bathroom. None of our teachers were fossils. We had found every class before the bell rang, and two girls, Kaitlin and Janelle, had asked us if we wanted to sit at their lunch table.

They were waiting outside the gym for us. "It's huge," I said when Janelle opened the door.

Kaitlin grinned. "Wait until you see the pool," she said.

Right before the bell rang, Ms. Page, our gym teacher, told us about the sports program. "I hope each one of you will go out for a team," she said. "See me after class for the sign-up papers."

"What are you going out for?" Ellie whispered.

"The swim team. If my mom and dad say it's okay."

Ellie slapped me a high five. "Me, too."

When I walked into the house, Agatha came bounding out from nowhere and rubbed against my leg. Nelia came to the top of the stairs and peered down. "You're home. Good," she said. "Did you have a good day?"

I nodded and said, "Guess what, if Mom and Dad say it's okay, I'm going to be on the swim team." Then I asked, "Where are they?"

"They're in Chicago, shopping for their trip. They'll be back soon."

"When are we having dinner?" My stomach was growling so loud Nelia heard it, too. We laughed.

"We'll eat when your parents get home, but for now there's fruit in the bowl on the kitchen table and your favorite cookies are in the pantry."

"Oreos?"

Nelia nodded. "I'll be right down, as soon as I save what I wrote," she said. "I want to hear all about school."

When Nelia came downstairs, I told her about meeting Kaitlin and Janelle at school. And then we talked about the swim team. "I hope Mom and Dad say I can join because it's going to be fun. Janelle told us the swimsuits are royal blue. But our name, the Dolphins, is in hot pink."

"I like that," Nelia said.

"Me, too. And guess what? We get goggles. But Ellie thinks she's going to buy her own. She wants the Swedish ones that fit over your eyeball."

"Is that what you want?" Nelia asked.

I shook my head and blinked my eyes. "Something on my eyeball would gross me out, so I'm going to stick with the regular kind."

"You're really excited about swimming, aren't you?" Nelia asked.

I nodded. "I'd swim all the time if I could. And I've never been on a school team."

While Nelia and I were talking, Mom and Dad called and said they wouldn't be home for dinner. Nelia and I decided to go out for hamburgers. When we came back, the van was in the driveway. Mom and Dad were sitting in it making out. Nelia beeped the horn just a little and waved.

Not me. I just pretended I didn't see them kissing.

"We had such a good time," Mom said as we walked into the house. While Mom was showing us the clothes she had bought, Dad asked me about school.

"It was okay." I told them about the Dolphins. "Can I sign up?"

Mom frowned and looked over at Dad. "I don't know, Loren," she said. "I'm not sure it's a good idea to get involved with a team. Why don't you just go swimming?"

"Swimming by myself would be boring. I was going to be on the team at Los Olas. Why can't I be a Dolphin?"

Mom and Dad looked at each other. They said something with their eyes but I couldn't tell what it was. Then Dad said, "I can't think of any reason except . . . your hair might turn green."

"Dad! Come on, be serious. Don't joke about my hair. Mom might believe you."

"Loren!" Mom laughed. "I know a joke when I hear one. If you want to be a Dolphin, sign up for the team."

The next morning at school, Ellie and I checked the announcement boards. Just as Ellie read aloud, "Dolphins will meet after school at the swimming pool," Janelle and Kaitlin came running up to us.

"We made it!" Janelle shouted.

"Did you guys?" Kaitlin asked.

Ellie and I nodded. "We're a team!"

·chapter five·

At the gym door, Kaitlin, Janelle, Ellie, and I handed our permission slips to the tall, blonde, pretty woman who was standing there. "That's Ms. Lyndstrom, our coach," Kaitlin whispered.

A few minutes later, Ms. Lyndstrom blew her whistle and we followed her to the pool. When she opened the door, we got a whiff of the good old chlorine smell. I wrinkled up my nose and so did Ellie. "I guess we'll get used to it," she said.

We sat in the bleachers and listened to Ms. Lyndstrom talk about the responsibilities of being a Dolphin. "Number one rule: Be at *all* practices. And I mean all. Three-thirty to five-thirty, Monday, Wednesday, and Friday. Any questions?"

Ellie raised her hand. "What if you *have* to miss a practice?"

"You'd better have a good excuse," Ms. Lyndstrom said. "And girls, getting your period isn't an excuse. It happens to everyone."

Ellie's face turned bright red, and so did her neck. Somebody gave a nervous little giggle. I think it was Kaitlin. I stared at the pace clock and hoped nobody would guess I didn't have my period, yet.

"Okay. On to rule number two." Ms. Lyndstrom smiled at us. "The *S* rule. No smoking. No swearing. No slackers. Everybody does the workout. Any questions?"

Nobody raised her hand. Ms. Lyndstrom nodded and continued. "Rule number three: Team spirit. Everybody works hard to improve their individual skills, but we score points for the Dolphins. And we cheer each other on. Got it?"

We all nodded. "Okay," Ms. Lyndstrom said. "Practice starts next Monday. We'll talk about the meets then. I'll see you in the locker room to sign up for suits."

As we stood up, Ms. Lyndstrom said, "Wait. One more rule. It doesn't apply to everyone. I'd like you all to wear bathing caps. However, if your hair touches your shoulders, you *must* wear a cap."

Ellie tugged on my ponytail. "That's you," she said as we headed toward the locker room.

"Hey, you guys, look." Kaitlin pointed to the showers. "My sister was right! No curtains!"

"I'm not taking a shower," I said.

"Me, either," Ellie agreed. "I don't like the bare butt look."

We all giggled. "Hey, guys," Kaitlin said, "we won't have a choice. My sister said Ms. Lyndstrom is always on shower patrol."

As we rode home, Ellie and I talked about being Dolphins. "My backstroke is pretty good," Ellie said.

"Mine is, too, but I like freestyle best," I told Ellie.

"Who do you think Ms. Lyndstrom will pick to be the distance swimmer?" Ellie asked, and then she answered her own question. "Maybe you. I can see you, going the distance."

"It might be fun," I said. "And I could do it. In Florida, I used to swim against the waves, and that's harder than swimming against time."

When we turned the corner, we spotted RJ and Nolan riding toward us. "Watch RJ," Ellie commanded. "As soon as he and Nolan get close to us, RJ's going to do something."

"Like what?"

"I don't know. Something stupid."

RJ pulled up close and started doing wheelies. Nolan did them, too. Ellie and I stopped riding and watched them raise their bikes high and plop them down again. Ellie clapped and said in a sticky-sweet voice, "You're so good, RJ. Isn't he good, Loren?"

RJ growled, "Bug off, Ellie." He didn't say anything to me.

"What's with RJ?" I asked.

"He's mad at me because I tease him about you."

"Me? Why?"

"RJ likes you."

I shook my head. "He does not."

"Oh yeah? Who do you think he was showing off for?"

I shrugged. "I don't know. No one. He was just having fun."

"Loren, are you living on another planet?"

"No, I'm not living on another planet. What makes you think he likes me?"

"I know RJ. He doesn't ask a zillion questions

about someone he doesn't like. And he spent fifteen minutes in the bathroom this morning combing his hair. RJ never combs his hair. He likes you!"

I laughed. "I don't think so. But I think Nolan likes you."

Ellie grinned. "Maybe."

The rest of the way home, Ellie and I talked about the team.

When I walked in the door, Mom called out, "Is that you, Loren? I'm in the garden room."

Mom was working on her painting. "Rimini called. He's going to meet your dad and me at the airport."

"When are you leaving?"

"Early tomorrow morning."

"I wish you didn't have to go."

"We'll be back soon—in time for your birthday."

"That's in December, Mom."

That night, after I had kissed everybody good night, Mom came in my room. "I thought I'd brush your hair before you went to bed," Mom said.

Mom brushed at least two hundred times.

When she finally finished, she put down my brush and walked over to my dollhouse. It's set on a low table in the far corner of my room.

"It's so much like Rimini's house," Mom said. She ran her fingers across the red roof and down the pale pink walls. She moved and changed something in each room. Then Mom said, "You know, Loren, the dollhouse was my twelfth birthday present from Rimini."

"I know, Mom." Every year on my birthday, Mom tells me how Rimini came to New York to see her on her twelfth birthday. It was the first time she had seen him since she was a little baby, which is pretty weird.

It's also more than a little weird, I thought, that I hadn't seen Rimini since I was a little kid. When I was four, Mom, Dad, and I went to Italy. We stayed at Rimini's house on the beach. All I remember is riding on his shoulders as he ran in and out of the waves.

That night, I dreamed I was floating across the ocean in my dollhouse. I was on my way to see Rimini.

The next day, when I came home from school, Mom and Dad were packed and ready to leave.

When the limo came to get them, Mom hugged me so hard I couldn't breathe. Dad held me tight, too. And then they were gone.

When I asked Nelia if I could go down to the lake, I thought she was going to say no, but she just said, "Don't stay too long."

I rode as fast as I could to the park. When I got there, I locked my bike and raced to the end of the pier.

As I was standing on the pier, watching the tiny whitecaps roll in, a giant wave of missing everybody washed over me. For a minute, I closed my eyes and just let the tears roll down my cheeks.

"Hey, Loren!"

I wiped my face and eyes with the back of my hands and turned around. Ellie was racing toward me. RJ and Nolan were right behind her.

"What are you guys doing here?" I asked.

"Looking for you," RJ said. "We went over to your house, and your grandmother said you rode your bike to the lake."

"What are you doing?" Nolan asked.

I shrugged. "Hanging out." It sounded too dumb to say, "I miss the ocean and that's why I'm here." And then, because I couldn't think of anything else to say, I said, "Race you to the shoreline!"

RJ won. When he and Nolan started skipping stones, Ellie said, "We can beat you guys."

"Want to bet?" Nolan asked.

"You're on!" Ellie and I shouted.

"Losers buy Slurpees," RJ said.

My first stone sank. RJ grinned and shook his head. "You can't throw just any stone. It has to be flat, like this." He handed me a stone.

"Thanks," I said. My stone skipped across the water, but not as far as everybody else's.

I looked for another one. It's not easy to find flat stones, but Ellie and I lucked out and found as many as the guys. As hard as we tried, though, our stones trailed behind. "We have to practice," Ellie said.

"It's giant Slurpee time for the champions!" Nolan said. He jabbed Ellie in the shoulder.

"Hey, next time, we'll win," I said. Ellie nodded.

"You didn't do too bad . . . Monroe . . . for a girl," RJ said.

"Thanks so very much," I said. "If my arms were as long as yours, I'd have won. Hands down."

49

Ellie grabbed RJ's arm. "Cheat! Cheat! We win! All monkey arms are disqualified."

RJ broke away, chattering, "Monkey man on the loose. Monkey man on the loose," and started chasing me. Nolan chased Ellie. I raced back out onto the pier, which was pretty dumb because there's nowhere to go when you get to the end. "Time out," I gasped.

The four of us flopped down at the end of the pier and caught our breath. "You run good for a girl," RJ teased.

I groaned, and Ellie smacked him on the arm with her baseball cap. For a while, we watched the waves roll in. "I miss swimming in the ocean," I said.

"You'll get to swim a lot when we're on the team," Ellie reminded me.

"Right," I said, and wished I could swim anywhere I wanted, anytime.

· chapter six ·

On the way home, we stopped at 7-Eleven. Nolan said they had the best Slurpees. "And it's right next to Marvel's," RJ said.

"What's Marvel's?" I whispered to Ellie.

"It's a comic book store. RJ's hooked on comic books. He collects them, draws them, and drives you crazy talking about them."

When we walked into 7-Eleven, Nolan said, "All right, you guys, fork over."

I whispered to Ellie, "All I have is fifty cents."

Ellie laughed. "I have a quarter. Okay, guys," she said, "here's the deal: We can buy one Slurpee. You have to split it."

"Cheap, cheap, cheap," Nolan said.

"Take it or leave it," Ellie said. "What do you want?"

"Cola," RJ said. Nolan nodded. They groaned when they saw the small cup. They gave it to Ellie and me and bought the monster ones for themselves.

When we finished, we went over to Marvel's. RJ bought two copies of the latest Spider-Man.

"Why did you buy two?" I asked.

"One's for saving," RJ said. He held up a comic book. "Hey, Nolan. This is a Todd McFarlane one."

"That's going to be big bucks someday," Nolan said.

"Who's Todd McFarlane?" I asked Ellie.

RJ overheard me and said, "He's the artist. I'm going to be like him someday."

"He will, too." Nolan put his arm across RJ's shoulders. "You'll see."

RJ rode next to me on the way home. I told him my mom was an artist. "What do you draw?" I asked.

RJ grinned. "Comics."

"I know that. Who do you draw?"

"Spider-Man, Superman, X-Men. But I have my own hero: James Roberts, the Shape Changer."

"What's a shape changer?"

"It's like this," RJ explained. "Roberts, a crime-fighting scientist, by accident discovered a formula that can change him into anything or anybody. He can be Agent 007 or Monkey Man."

"Or Chicken Man," Ellie said as she rode up next to me.

"Shut up, Ellie," RJ said. He rode on ahead.

When I came home, I found Nelia in her office typing away. She asked if RJ, Nolan, and Ellie had found me. I nodded.

"Good," Nelia said. "I thought they'd track you down. Are you hungry?"

When I shook my head, she said, "Okay. Maybe we'll have pizza later."

Nelia took off her reading glasses and rubbed her eyes. "I'll finish this chapter. It's a tough one. I'm afraid Mrs. Gilman is going to walk right into the killer's trap." She smiled and asked, "What are you going to do?"

"I'm going to start on my family-tree project for social studies," I told her. Agatha followed me upstairs, but I didn't pay any attention to her.

I tried to do my homework, but when your brain shuts down, you really don't care who your great-grandparents are. You really don't care about anything.

The only thing I felt like doing was rearranging the furniture in my dollhouse. I put everything back the way it was before Mom changed it.

At six o'clock, Nelia knocked on my door. When I opened it, she said, "I could eat a pizza. What about you?"

I shrugged. Nelia said, "If you can live with onions, I can live without mushrooms."

"Onions are okay," I said. I picked up Agatha, who had curled up on the rug, and rubbed my forehead against hers. She jumped out of my arms when my tears fell on her nose.

I stopped crying when Nelia put her arms around me. "Do you want to talk about it?" she asked.

"No," I whispered into her chest.

"Loren, I know how hard it can be to say good-bye," Nelia whispered back. "Whenever you feel like talking, I'm here."

"I know," I said.

That night, when I couldn't sleep, I thought about getting up and going to Nelia's room. I knew she'd make room for me in her bed; she did when Mom and Dad were gone before. But . . . I was just a little kid then. Instead, I listened to my

Seals tape. You can hear the sound of the waves when they sing "Ocean Blues."

The next day, Ms. Lyndstrom smiled at Ellie and me when we paid for our suits and goggles. She said, "See you Monday at practice."

Riding home from school, Ellie and I talked about being a Dolphin and about guys. "Do you like RJ?" Ellie asked.

"Do you like Nolan?" I asked.

"No fair. I asked you first."

I shrugged. "I don't know."

Did I like RJ? Maybe yes. Maybe no. I was so busy trying to decide, as I rode down the driveway, that I almost didn't see Nelia getting into her car. "How was school?" she asked.

I shrugged and said, "I have a ton of homework. Where are you going?"

"To my pottery class. We're working with color. I'm doing a turquoise bowl." Before Nelia started the car she asked, "Any chance you might be hungry?"

"I'm starving!"

Nelia laughed. "Good. There are DoveBars in the freezer. And there's ham in the refrigerator if you want to make a sandwich."

"When are you going to be home?"

Nelia said, "By six-thirty at the latest. I'll bring back dinner. How about hamburgers, fries, and chocolate milk shakes?"

"Sounds good to me." We order out a lot because Nelia says cooking is not one of her contributions to society.

I waved to her as she backed the car down the driveway. Halfway down, she stopped and poked her head out the car window. "Loren!" she called to me, "I forgot to tell you, there's a letter for you in the mail basket on the hall table."

"It must be from Stephanie," I said. It was. I sat at the kitchen table, ate a DoveBar, looked at the pictures Stephanie sent, and read her letter three times.

Hi Loren,

Sorry I haven't called but my mom has a thing about long-distance calls. I miss you more than a lot.

Do you remember Michelle White, the girl with the short red hair and a ton of freckles? In case you don't, she's the one who tried to teach us to do a backward flip on the balance beam. Well, anyway, Michelle and I are hanging out together now.

We sit next to each other in Dreiser's class. But

guess what, Dreiser's not that bad. Keep it a secret but I sort of like her. And you'll never believe this, I'm starting to like math too. Pretty weird, huh?

October 3, if there isn't a hurricane, the Kid's Triathlon is going to be in Los Olas. 500 kids are coming. I wish you were one of them. Michelle, you and I could do a three-way relay team. Michelle could run, she has the longest legs, I could bike and you could swim. We'd win for sure.

Have to go now. Call me or write. SOON! And I mean SOON!

Your best friend forever,

Stephanie

P.S. Aren't the pictures cool?

P.P.S. How's school for you?

P.P.P.S. Thought you might want to know, it's the same old same old with the guys down here. Carl and Alec are the only cool ones. And they're too busy playing soccer to know anybody is alive.

P.P.P.P.S. What about RJ? Do you like him?

Why is everybody asking me if I like RJ?

•chapter seven•

The next two weeks flew by. I talked to Mom and Dad three times, did tons of homework, and practiced, practiced, practiced for the first swimming meet.

Right before the meet, Ellie and I were bobbing up and down in the deep end of the pool. I bobbed under and came shooting up. Ellie laughed. "You look like a conehead," she said.

"It's my hair. I really had to stuff it into the cap."

"Swimmers, take your mark!" a voice boomed over the loudspeaker.

Ellie and I scrambled up out of the water and onto the blocks. At the sound of the gun, *splash!*

into the water and off. Fast. Fast. Faster. It's only fifty yards.

"Good job," Ellie said, slapping me a wet high five when we climbed out of the pool. "I bet we're winning."

Chrystal Hunter, Patty Nelson, two other Dolphins I didn't know, and Ellie and I sat on the bench and chanted, "go, go, go" as Kaitlin swam the fifty-yard backstroke relay.

"Everybody out of the water! Get out! Get out!" one of the timers yelled.

"What's going on?" I asked Ellie.

She shrugged. Janelle came running up to us, holding her nose. "Somebody threw up, right in the pool!" she yelled.

Kaitlin, dripping wet, ran over to us. "Can you believe it? Puke in the water! Ugh!"

"Major gross-out," I said.

Everybody agreed. "At least I made my points," Kaitlin said, as she wrapped herself up in a towel.

Ten minutes later, we were still sitting around waiting for the extra chlorine to do its job. "My stomach is doing the fly," Ellie said.

"Mine has butterflies, too," Kaitlin said. "What if we both throw up?"

"Focus on swimming, Dolphins," Ms. Lyndstrom said. "We're racking up the points."

Ms. Lyndstrom gave each of us pointers for our events. "Loren," she said, "ride high in the water, don't let your legs sink. That will help the drag."

The next event was the freestyle relay. Janelle, Kaitlin, Ellie, and I were swimming as a team. We were neck and neck with the Racers when it happened. Rip! My bathing cap split.

Forget it, faster, faster, I told myself, but when you have hair in your face, and every time you take a side breath you breathe in a mouthful of hair, it's hopeless.

Because of me, we didn't make any points. "Sorry, guys," I said.

After the meet, Ms. Lyndstrom stopped me. "You'll have another chance to swim against the Racers, Loren. You did better than okay today."

"Of all the dumb luck," I said to Ellie on the way home, "my cap had to split open."

"You looked like the monster from the deep." Ellie laughed.

"Thank you very much. My monster hair cost us points."

"Why don't you get it cut?"

"Do you want to see me dead and buried? If I

snipped off one tiny piece of my hair, my mom would kill me."

"She's not here. And anyway, if you cut off a little bit, maybe she wouldn't notice when she gets back."

"My mom would notice."

That night, after I finished my homework, I asked Nelia if I could call Ellie. Ellie didn't answer the phone, RJ did. "This is the Blake house. RJ speaking."

A weird thing happened when I heard RJ's voice. My heart gave a flutter kick. "Hi," I squeaked. "It's me, Loren. Is Ellie there?'

"Not really," RJ said. "She was in the shower so long, she turned into a dolphin. We're trying to get the aquarium to accept her."

I couldn't help it, I laughed.

"Is that for me?" Ellie shouted.

"Nope," RJ shouted back. "Dolphins never get phone calls."

"You guys!" I shouted into the phone. "Talk to me."

"RJ, give me the phone," I heard Ellie scream. "Loren is that you?" she asked.

When I said yes, Ellie said, "Hold on." She shouted, "If you don't leave me alone, RJ, I'm telling!" There was a pause, then Ellie said, "He's gone."

When I started to ask where, Ellie interrupted me. "I can't believe you called. I was going to call you. Guess what, guess what!"

"What?"

"RJ's sleeping over at Nolan's house next Saturday night, so my mom said I can have a sleepover here. Can you come?'

"I think so, but I have to ask."

"Hurry up and find out. I'm going to ask Janelle and Kaitlin."

After we hung up, I went into the living room to find Nelia. She was curled up on the couch watching *Mystery*. When I told her about Ellie's sleepover, she said it sounded like fun.

The next morning, while I was pouring my cereal into a bowl, the phone rang. It was Mom. Every time I hear Mom or Dad's voice, I go all mushy inside. "Loren, I miss you so much," Mom said.

"I miss you and Dad, too," I said. Before I went into major mush, Mom asked, "Do you know what?"

Sometimes Mom asks silly questions. I laughed and said, "No. What?"

"I have a wonderful surprise."

Surprises can smack you in the face like a high-breaking wave. I thought for sure Mom and Dad were coming home early, before my birthday. They weren't.

The big surprise was, Rimini was coming back with them. And he wanted Mom and me to be his models for a book of fairy tales. Who has time to be Sleeping Beauty? I'm not going to do it. I'm not going to be anybody but me.

When Nelia walked into the kitchen she said, "I heard the phone ring. Who was it?"

I shoved my bowl of cornflakes across the table and muttered, "Mom."

Nelia handed me a paper towel to wipe up the spilled milk. "Do you want to talk about what's bothering you?"

I told Nelia what was going on. "Even if Rimini is my grandfather, and it's a big deal honor to pose for him, I don't want to do it. I don't know him."

Nelia sat down at the table. She said, "You'll have to talk about your feelings with your mom and dad. Promise me you will?"

I nodded, but I kept my head down and drew circles on the kitchen table with my finger.

"What else is bothering you, Loren?"

I looked up at Nelia. "Mom said she has another surprise. But she wouldn't tell me what it is. I hate surprises, Nelia."

Nelia smiled at me. "Surprises can be good or bad. Once my brother told me he had put a special surprise in my lunch box. I thought it was the giant Hershey bar I saw on his dresser, but it was a long green garden snake."

"Aargh. Didn't you almost croak?"

"Almost. But I surprised my brother. I pretended nothing happened, and that night, I put the snake under his pillow."

"Did you really do that, Nelia?"

Nelia nodded. "Those were bad surprises, but your coming here was a good surprise. It was not only a surprise, it was a wish come true."

"You wished for me?"

"On every star I saw," Nelia said.

"I'm going to wish we stay here," I said.

·chapter eight·

All the way to school, Ellie and I planned what we'd do at the sleepover. I suggested flashlight tag.

Ellie didn't know what it was, so I explained it to her. "Last year, Stephanie, my best friend in Los Olas, had a sleepover and we played it. It's fun. Whoever is It tags players with the light beam."

When we got to school, Ellie asked Kaitlin and Janelle if they ever played the game. "It's kissing tag here," Janelle said.

"Are you serious?" I asked.

Janelle nodded. "Last year I chased Daniel Smythe around the block."

"Did you catch him?" I asked.

65

"No," Janelle answered. "But if I did, it probably would have been a bad kissing experience. My sister told me his brother has dog breath, so Daniel probably has it, too."

All of us decided it would be more fun if the guys weren't around, anyway. "RJ's spending the night at Nolan's," Ellie said. "Which is probably a good thing. If RJ, Nolan, and their friends came over, we'd probably end up in the middle of a Super-Soaker war."

"So what are we going to do?" I asked.

"I have a good idea," Janelle said. "We could do makeovers."

"Cool," Ellie said. "We did them when I lived in Washington."

"What should we bring?" Kaitlin asked.

"Bring nail polish and makeup," Ellie said.

Janelle added, "Don't forget shaving cream, Daisy razors, tweezers, and magazines. *Beautiful You* has an article called 'Ten Steps to a New Look.' And some hot, hot ads."

At lunch, Ellie, Janelle, Kaitlin, and I made more plans for the sleepover. We decided we'd go for tag, do the makeovers, design our own Dolphin T-shirts and pig out on pizza, popcorn, and s'mores. Kaitlin said she knew how to make s'mores in the microwave.

After school, I asked Nelia if Mom had called. When Nelia said yes, I asked her if Mom and Dad had changed their plans. Deep inside, even though I knew it was stupid, I was hoping they were coming home before my birthday, without Rimini.

"Your mother said they're still working on their plans," Nelia replied in a soft voice. Then Nelia got up from her desk, came over to me, and gave me a big hug. She held me extra tight. "I needed that hug," she said.

Later on, while I was playing with Agatha, the phone rang. It was Ellie. We talked about the sleepover again until Ellie's mom came home and made her get off the phone.

After dinner, I wrote to Stephanie. I knew she'd want to know what was going on.

Hi Stephanie,

Big news. Ellie is having a sleepover. I think we'll have fun but the most fun I ever had was at your sleepover last year.

Do you still watch the video we made? I still

crack up when I think how Haley imitated Big Bird meeting Mr. Rogers. Maybe she'll get a job on Sesame Street.

Did you get you-know-what yet? I didn't. My grandmother says not to worry, she didn't get her period until she was thirteen. I hope I don't have to wait that long. But I wouldn't mind waiting until swimming season is over. Getting "it" right in the middle of a meet would be worse than getting a cramp in the middle of a relay race.

It's really fun being a Dolphin. Our next swimming meet is the same day as your triathlon. Maybe we'll both be swimming at the same time. I wish we were on the same team just like we had planned.

By the next meet, I have to figure out a way to keep my hair from being a real drag. I wish my mom would let me cut it. Sometimes I wonder if she'd notice if I had more than the ends trimmed. Right now I'm too chicken to find out.

Can you believe it, right before my parents left for Europe, I got my first zit, a humongous red one right at the end of my nose. One of the guys at school who thinks he's really cool but is really a Neanderthal asked me if I was going to substitute for Rudolph on Christmas eve. I pretended I didn't hear him.

Have you talked to Carl or Alec yet? RJ and I talk. Sometimes I think maybe I like him back. But I don't know if I'm ready to have a relationship with anyone. All that kissing and stuff. What do you think?

If I didn't know better I'd think my dollhouse was haunted. When I woke up the other morning all the lamps, two paintings and the kitchen dishes were on the floor. Nelia says Agatha's curiosity got the better of her, or the house was in a settling mood.

I hope she's right. Who wants a haunted dollhouse in their bedroom? Next Sunday Nelia is taking me to the Art Institute. They have a miniature room collection. I need some new ideas for my Christmas room.

My mom says she has a surprise for me. So if I'm lucky, the surprise will be all my birthday wishes will come true. One of my wishes is that you'll come here for a visit.

Another wish is that all of us including Nelia will visit Los Olas. You'll like my grandmother. She's cool. Did I tell you she bought another bike?

We ride down to the lake after dinner if I don't have too much homework.

It's getting late, almost ten o'clock so I better stop. Say "hi" to Haley for me.

Write and tell me what's going on. SOON! I miss you more than a lot.

Your best friend forever,

Loren

P.S. Loved the pictures. Thanks.

P.P.S. I'll write and tell you about the sleepover.

Early Saturday morning, the phone rang. It was Ellie. "What's up?" I asked.

"It's ruined. Everything is ruined."

"What are you talking about?" I asked, trying not to yawn.

"RJ's going to be home tonight," she said.

"Why? I thought he was going to Nolan's."

"He was, but Nolan's parents won a getaway weekend so Nolan's getting away at my house."

"What are we going to do?"

"My mom says the guys can pitch a tent in the yard or sleep in the basement. Can you believe it? Mom promised me they won't bother us. Ha, ha! Come prepared."

When I got over to Ellie's house, Janelle and Kaitlin were already there. "We're going to sleep in my bedroom," Ellie said.

"Where are the guys?" Kaitlin asked.

"Why do you care?" Janelle teased.

"I don't care. I was just curious," Kaitlin answered. She plopped her overnight bag down on the floor.

"We're safe for now. Nolan and RJ are at the show with my dad," Ellie said.

"Okay, guys," Janelle said, "you have to see what I brought." Janelle hauled out her hair dryer, curling iron, a stack of five magazines, a makeup case, two cans of shaving cream, deodorant, a pair of scissors, tweezers, a hair brush and comb, and a one-eyed teddy bear. "I never go anywhere without Sam," she said.

Kaitlin was next. The first thing she took out of her overnight bag was a giant jar of M&M's. Then she said, "Look at this, if the guys come, we're prepared."

"With a calculator?" I asked.

"Let me show you," Kaitlin said. She squirted a stream of water at Ellie, Janelle, and me. "Squirt!" she yelled. Ellie got it right in the face.

"I have one, too. Look!" Janelle handed me two

packages of gum. "Squeeze it." Cold water hit me in the neck.

"Is that cool or is that cool?" Janelle asked.

"Cool," I answered, as I wiped my neck.

"Put a piece of the other one in your mouth," Janelle said.

"Not me," I said.

"Don't be chicken." Janelle grabbed a piece of gum. It turned her mouth blue.

Everybody cracked up. "Let's hope we get a chance to show the guys," Kaitlin said.

Ellie grinned. "Okay," she said. "Sit down. Listen, so it doesn't get boring, we have to plan what we're going to do."

Before we could decide what to do first, Ellie whispered, "Stop, don't say a word." She crawled over to the door, reached up and yanked it open. RJ and Nolan were standing outside.

"Disappear, you guys," Ellie hissed.

"I live here, too," RJ said.

Ellie stood up and went chin to chin with RJ. "If you don't go to the basement, I'm telling."

"I'm telling," RJ mocked. He and Nolan pushed past Ellie and stood over us. "Are you going to tell Dad I just came upstairs for my flashlight?"

"How about these M&M's?" Nolan shouted, grabbing Kaitlin's jar.

"Hey," Kaitlin said. "Hands off."

RJ grabbed Sam, Janelle's teddy bear, and said, "Catch us if you can."

The four of us raced down the stairs and out of the house after the guys. The streetlights were on. We chased RJ and Nolan around the block, but we didn't catch them. They disappeared right in front of my house. "Where are they?" I whispered.

Whoosh! Right in the face. RJ and Nolan came leaping out from behind a tree. It was a one-sided Super-Soaker war.

"I'm going for the shaving cream!" Janelle screamed.

"I'll hold them off." I ran to the side of the house and tried to turn on Nelia's hose.

By the time Janelle and Kaitlin returned, Ellie and I were soaked. So were RJ and Nolan. "Got you!" Janelle sprayed shaving cream on RJ.

He grabbed the can away from Janelle but we chased them into the backyard, yelling and screaming.

Mr. and Mrs. Blake, Ellie and RJ's parents, came out. They made us turn in the shaving cream, and the guys had to hand over their Super Soakers.

The guys went to the basement to clean up. We dried off in the kitchen and then headed upstairs to Ellie's bedroom. It took me forever to dry my hair.

Janelle brushed it out. "How do you get all this hair in your swimming cap?" Janelle asked.

"I shove it in and pray my cap stretches far enough. Ellie pulls it down in the back for me. It's a drag."

When we walked into the kitchen, RJ and Nolan were pigging out on pizza. "It's a good thing we decided to wear sweats instead of night-shirts," I whispered to Ellie.

"Where are my M&M's?" Kaitlin asked.

"And where's Sam?" Janelle asked.

RJ grinned. "Only the Shape Changer knows."

"You are such a dork, RJ," Ellie said.

"Okay," Kaitlin said, "how do we find out from the Shape Changer?"

"Kaitlin," Ellie said, "don't give in to them."

"But what if I have an M&M attack during the night?"

"The Shape Changer can help you . . . for a small fee," Nolan said out of the side of his mouth.

"What's the price?" I asked.

"Divvy up the M&M's," RJ said. He walked over to me and pulled on my ponytail. "You come with me."

"Me?"

RJ grinned. "The Shape Changer has spoken."

"If you bring Loren and Sam back in the same shape, we'll throw in some gum," Janelle said.

"Thanks a great big heap, guys," I said as I followed RJ out the door.

·chapter nine·

The beam of RJ's flashlight made a path across the grass. "Where are we going?" I asked.

"Behind the garage. That's where we hid the M&M's and Sam," RJ said.

"Why did you want me to come with you?" I asked RJ.

"No reason," he said. We picked up Sam, who was pretty soggy, and the M&M jar. Neither of us said anything. If I had a brother, maybe I'd know why guys act more then weird sometimes.

Right before we got to the deck, RJ stopped and said, "*Spider-Man*'s at Cinema 2. Want to go to-morrow?"

"I don't know. Maybe. I'll have to ask. Who's going?"

"Me. Nolan and Ellie."

"Ellie didn't say anything to me."

"Nolan didn't ask her yet. He'll probably ask her tomorrow." RJ beamed the light at the stairs. "So if I call you tomorrow . . . will you know?"

"If, and it's a big *if,* I can reach my parents. They're in Italy with my grandfather."

"So what's the big deal about Italy?"

"Have you ever tried to call there? It takes forever to get through and then there's the time difference. When it's seven o'clock here, it's two o'clock in the morning there."

"Ask your grandmother, if you don't get hold of your Mom and Dad."

When we walked in the door, RJ said to Nolan, "Mission accomplished." He held up the M&M's jar.

Nolan slapped him a high five. "Okay guys," he said, "divvy up the M&M's."

Kaitlin divided them and then Janelle picked up Sam and said, "Here's your gum." We left the kitchen . . . walking out very casually.

We raced up to Ellie's bedroom. "Close the door!" Ellie shouted. We put her chair up against the doorknob and collapsed on the floor. "I wish I could see RJ with blue teeth," Ellie said.

RJ and Nolan came running up the stairs. "Revenge will be ours!" they shouted.

When they pounded on the door, we heard Ellie's dad bark, "Into the basement, boys. Now!"

After we settled down, Janelle asked, "Why did RJ ask you to go outside with him?"

"I know! I know!" Ellie shrieked. "Because he likes her."

"Did he kiss you?" Kaitlin asked.

I threw my pillow at her and that started a pillow fight. Ellie chased me around the room chanting, "Tell, tell, tell."

"He didn't kiss me. . . . He asked me out . . . to the show."

"I bet you any money he'll kiss you. Are you going to let him?"

"That's for me to know . . . and nobody to find out."

Janelle laughed. "Hey, if you just might be making out, don't you want a makeover?"

Ellie picked up *Beautiful You* and handed it to me. "Read this, Loren—'The Wow Brow.' "

I read it. "I guess bushy eyebrows are out."

"Look at mine," Janelle said. She ran her finger

over her right eyebrow. "The arch is in. We could give you a whole new look."

"How?" I asked.

"I'll tweeze your eyebrows," Janelle said.

"And I can cut your hair," Kaitlin said. "I trim my Mom's bangs all the time."

"Cut my hair?" I grabbed hold of my ponytail. "I don't know, guys. I don't think so."

At breakfast the next morning, just as I was biting into my chocolate doughnut, RJ walked into the kitchen. When he saw me, he frowned. "What did you do to your face?" he asked.

"Nothing. Why?"

RJ shrugged, squinted up his eyes, and stared. Finally he said, "Your eyebrow, the right one, changed shape. It's lopsided."

I covered my eyebrow with my hand.

"Loren's eyebrow is arched," Ellie said.

"Looks crooked to me," Nolan said.

Janelle, Ellie, and Kaitlin told me the guys didn't know one eyebrow from another. "They never read *Beautiful You*," Kaitlin said.

"Your eyebrows look good," Janelle insisted.

When I got home, I flew up the stairs calling, "Nelia, Nelia, where are you?"

Nelia came out of the bathroom. She had her

toothbrush in her hand. "Did you have a goo— what happened to your eyebrows?"

"Janelle tweezed them."

Nelia nodded. "I think we need a little repair work here."

I sat on the edge of Nelia's bed while she drew a new shape over my eyebrows with her eyebrow pencil. She pulled out all the hairs that were outside the line. No matter how much it hurt, I didn't say anything.

"That's better," Nelia said as she brushed my brows with a little black brush. "But I'd let them grow back just a little bit. The natural look is always in."

"Do you think Mom's going to kill me?" I asked, as I examined my new look in the mirror.

"I'm sure your Mom wouldn't want you to go through life with crooked eyebrows," Nelia said. "And they'll grow back before your birthday."

"I guess I'd be in big trouble if Mom and Dad came home early."

"I wouldn't worry about that," Nelia said. She walked over and picked up Agatha, who was meowing at the door. "Hush, cat," Nelia said, then she looked at me. "I want to hear all about the sleepover," she said.

Agatha, Nelia, and I sat on Nelia's bed while I told Nelia about the water fight and RJ. "Can I go to the show with RJ?" I asked.

Nelia laughed. "No fair, Loren, you know I can't make that decision." I made a pout face. Nelia put her finger on my lips. "You have to ask your mom and dad."

"I know." I snuggled a little closer to Nelia. "Don't tell, but I almost let Kaitlin cut my hair. But just as she was going to snip off a piece, I chickened out."

Nelia pulled on my ponytail and said, "Chickening out was using good judgment, Loren. I don't imagine Kaitlin has much hair-cutting experience."

"I really do want to cut my hair, Nelia."

"Tell your mom how you feel."

I shook my head. "Mom doesn't hear what I'm saying. And if I push, she'll either get that hurt look on her face or she'll get really mad."

"I know your problem," Nelia said softly.

"Do you think I have to tell Mom what *almost* happened?"

While Nelia was saying, "I don't think almost happened counts," the phone rang. I thought maybe it was Mom or Dad, but it was Ellie.

Nelia said, "Go ahead and talk. I'm going to take Agatha downstairs. She thinks it's tuna time."

"Did Nolan ask you?" I asked Ellie.

"Yes. Yes. Yes."

"What did you say?"

"I told him I'd go if you could go. So are you going to go?"

"I have to ask my mom."

"Your mom. She's in Europe. How are you going to ask her?"

"I have to call her up."

"Let me know as soon as you find out."

The phone rang in Italy nine times before Mom answered.

"Where were you?" I asked.

"In the garden. It's still warm here. It's so good to hear your voice, Loren. We were just talking about you," Mom said.

"You were? What did you say?"

Mom laughed. "We were discussing your school and my old school. I was telling your dad and Rimini how much I loved the Claremont Academy. We were wondering how you like Lake Shore?"

"It's okay."

"Just okay?"

"I like it, it's just that sometimes I miss Hemingway. And I guess I miss Hemingway because I miss Stephanie."

"Well you can always write to Stephanie and talk to her, once in a while. You make friends easily, Loren," Mom said. "By the way, how are RJ and Ellie?"

"Good," I told Mom. "Ellie had a sleepover. We pigged out on popcorn, pizza, and M&M's, watched MTV, danced to B96, and talked about being a Dolphin." All of which was true. I just didn't tell Mom *everything* we did.

"It sounds like you had a wonderful time," Mom said. "You know when I was at Claremont *every night* was like a sleepover."

I didn't say anything, but I wondered why Mom was making such a big deal about her old boarding school.

Mom and I talked for a few more minutes. She told me the critics like *Loren in the Garden.* I told her we were doing a family tree in social studies. Mom didn't act too thrilled about my project. She said she missed me and then she said, "Here's your dad."

"Mom wait, I have to ask you something."

She was gone. "Big news," Dad said. "Joel Williams is going to record my new song."

"What's it called?"

"'Seashells.'"

"Will they play it on B96?"

Dad laughed and said, "Probably not. I'll send you a tape. And I want you to know . . . Are you ready for this?"

"Ready for what?"

"I wrote it for *you*."

"You did? How? When? Where?"

Dad laughed again. "I was walking along the beach, and I found this very unusual shell. And I thought about you. While I was thinking about you, a song popped into my head."

"That really is cool, Dad. I miss you. I miss Mom, too."

"She's right here. She wants to talk to you again."

"Good. I have to ask her something." I figured if I asked Dad about the show, he'd say, ask your mom.

Before I could ask Mom, she said, "Loren, your grandfather wants to say hello," and then she was gone again.

"My little Loren, how are you?"

"Okay, how are you?"

Rimini laughed. "I'm okay, too. And I'm looking forward to seeing you soon. I told your mother, I think you will make a beautiful Rapunzel."

"Rapunzel? Is that the story of the girl with the long hair?"

"Yes. That is it. Your mother tells me you have beautiful long golden hair."

Oh great. Just great. Now I'll never be able to get my hair cut. Rimini went on talking about how wonderful it would be to paint Mom and me. Finally I asked him if I could talk to Mom again.

When Mom got back on the phone, I said, "Ellie, Nolan, and RJ are going to the movies this afternoon." Mom didn't say anything. "Can I go?"

I crossed my fingers as hard as I could and waited. I figured I didn't have to tell Mom that RJ personally asked me. Mom said yes right away. "Thanks Mom! Thanks!"

"It must be a good show. You sound excited," Mom said.

"*Spider-Man* is supposed to be even better than *Batman*," I told Mom.

"I don't know about spiders and bats," Mom said.

"Oh, Mom!"

Mom laughed. "I miss you, Loren. I'll talk to you soon. I need to talk to Nelia now."

Nelia took the phone upstairs and went into her office. I wondered why she closed the door. I decided to ask her as soon as she hung up. But when Nelia hung up, the phone rang right away. Nelia came out of her study and said, "It's for you, Loren. It's RJ."

The first thing RJ said to me was, "Can you go to the show?" When I said yes, he said, "It starts at two-thirty."

"How are we going to get there?"

"It's too far to walk, so we'll have to ride our bikes." RJ started to hang up.

"Wait, I need to talk to Ellie."

When Ellie picked up the phone, I told her Mom had said yes.

Ellie laughed. "I know. I could tell by the way RJ was grinning when he handed me the phone. Wait until I tell you."

"Tell me what."

Ellie whispered so low I could hardly hear

her, "RJ and Nolan are trying to decide . . . if they should . . . kiss us . . . at the show."

"Kiss? Us? Are you serious? How do you know?"

"I hid and listened to their conversation."

"What are we going to do?" I didn't know if I was ready to kiss RJ.

·chapter ten·

I brushed my teeth five times, flossed, and swished minty green mouthwash until my cheeks tingled. Then I blew my breath into my hand and sniffed. I still didn't know if I'd pass the "kissing sweet" test. How can you ask your grandmother if you have bad breath? How can you ask anyone?

And what if RJ has onion breath? Why can't we just go to the show? Why do we have to kiss? I don't know if I like RJ enough to kiss him.

Right before we left for the show, I brushed my teeth again. When RJ, Ellie, and Nolan rang the doorbell, I popped a mint in my mouth, said good-bye to Nelia and ran out the door. To kiss or not to kiss was still the big question.

We rode our bikes to Cinema 2. After we locked up, the guys charged for the line. Ellie and I followed them. We wondered if RJ and Nolan would pay our way. They didn't.

When we walked into the lobby, RJ said, "You guys get the seats, Nolan and I'll get the popcorn. Do you want butter, Loren?"

I nodded. Ellie and I found seats in the middle. "How should we sit?" I asked.

"Together."

"I know that. But what about the guys?"

"They'll figure it out."

"What are you going to do? Are you going to kiss Nolan?"

Ellie shrugged. "I don't know. What are you going to do?'

"I think I'm going to chicken out and just say no."

"Me, too," Ellie said. "I don't want my brother watching me kiss somebody."

"Can you believe it?" Ellie whispered to me when RJ and Nolan scrunched down in their seats. RJ and Nolan didn't sit next to us, they sat in *front* of us. After they handed us our popcorn, Ellie put her mouth to my ear and whispered, "They're more chicken than we are." We both clapped our hands over our mouths so we wouldn't laugh out loud.

On the way home, RJ rode next to me. "So, how did you like *Spider-Man*?" I asked.

"It was cool. But I thought his costume was pretty fake. I bet you any money Stan Lee and Larry Libber didn't like it either."

"Who are they?"

"They're the guys who drew the original Spider-Man." All the way home, RJ talked about Spider-Man, his favorite comic book, art, and his hero, the Shape Changer.

"Where did you get the name James Roberts?" I asked.

RJ grinned. "I named him after me. My real name is Robert James. I just did a switch-around."

"I wish I could switch my name around."

"If you could, what would it be?" RJ asked.

"Andrietta Loren."

RJ shook his head. "Nah! You don't look like an Andrietta. What's wrong with Loren?"

"It's a guy's name when it's spelled with an *o*. Lauren with an *au* is a girl's name. I was named after my grandfather, Loren Rimini."

"No kidding," RJ said. "I was named after my grandfather, too. Ellie was named after my grandmother. Don't tell her I told you, but Ellie's real name is *Eleanor.*"

Lucky Ellie, I thought. Eleanor is almost as bad as Loren, but at least Ellie got to change her name.

When Nolan, Ellie, RJ, and I got to my house, Nelia was waiting on the front porch. "See you guys," I said. And then I called after RJ, "Thanks for the popcorn."

Nelia didn't ask me about the show or anything; she said, "Loren, you have to call your mother."

"Now? It's after midnight in Italy."

"I know," Nelia said quietly. "But your mom and dad want you to call."

"Why? Is something wrong?"

Nelia shook her head and put her arm across my shoulders as we walked into the house. "I talked to your mom about an hour ago and . . . they just want to talk to you."

Something very, very weird was going on. Nelia's too quiet, I thought. And her eyes are all puffy and red. "Something has to be wrong," I said. "You've been crying."

Nelia gave my shoulder a squeeze. "You're being a little worrywart. I'm probably getting a cold. Go and call your parents."

I didn't believe Nelia, but there was nothing I

could do but call Mom and Dad. It took me a while to get through, but I finally did. After I talked to them, I couldn't figure out why Nelia had been crying. Mom was going to be home on Friday. She said the reason I had to call was she couldn't wait to tell me the good news.

I ran up the stairs to find Nelia. She was writing on her computer. "Nelia, Mom's going to be home Friday. She'll be here for my meet on Saturday."

"I know," Nelia said. "I didn't want to spoil the surprise."

"Boy, this time, the surprise was a good one," I said. "I wish Dad could come, too, but Mom told me this is just a quickie trip. She has to go to New York and then she's coming home for three days."

While we were eating dinner, Italian beef sandwiches from Jake's, I asked Nelia if she knew why Mom and Dad didn't tell me right away. "When I was talking to them this afternoon, they didn't say anything."

Nelia put her sandwich down and took a sip of her ginger ale. Then she said, "Your mom told me they made plans after they talked to you."

"Why is Mom going to New York?"

Nelia frowned, raised her eyebrows, and said,

"I can't answer your question, Loren. You will have to ask your mother when she gets here on Friday."

The way Nelia said "your mother," I knew something was going on. "Are you mad at Mom?" I asked.

"Why would you think that?"

I shrugged. "You're acting funny."

"I always act a little off balance when I'm getting a cold," Nelia said. If I didn't know Nelia better, I would think she was telling me a big fat lie.

Nelia changed the subject and asked me if I wanted to go down in the basement and throw a pot.

"Excuse me?" Why was Nelia acting so totally weird? "Do you throw pots like you throw darts?" I asked.

Nelia laughed. "No," she said. "I haven't really lost my mind. Come on, I'll show you."

As we were going down the stairs into the basement, Nelia said, "I bought a pottery wheel today while you were at the show."

I touched the wheel. "How does it work?" I asked.

"You put the clay on a wheel—that's throwing

the pot—and the shape emerges." Nelia smiled at me. "Your hands shape it, too."

While we were molding and smoothing miniature bowls for my dollhouse, Nelia and I talked about school, the movie, the Dolphins and Nelia's new book, *Hide and Seek*. We didn't talk about Mom and Dad.

Before I went to sleep, I marked the day off on the calendar. Every night, I marked off another day.

On Thursday night, I put a red ring around Friday. "Mom's coming home tomorrow," I said to Agatha, who was curled up on my pillow.

Just before I turned off my light, Nelia came to my room. She sat down on the side of my bed. "How much you have grown, Loren," she said. Then she looked over at my dollhouse. "Pretty soon, you'll be giving up your dollhouse."

"I'm not that big," I protested. "I'll still have it when I'm old. My grandkids can play with it."

Nelia smiled, brushed my hair away from my face, and kissed me good night.

•chapter eleven•

Nelia and I were at the gate when Mom's plane landed. As soon as I saw her, I raced over and gave her my best hug. Mom held me tight and said, "I missed you."

"I missed you, too," I whispered in her ear. "Big time."

On the way to the car, Mom said, "I didn't eat much on the plane, so how about if I treat for dinner?"

While we were waiting for our hamburgers, Nelia excused herself and went to the bathroom. Mom said, "Let me take a good look at you."

I turned to look at Mom, and she practically screamed. "What happened to your eyebrows?"

"Janelle tweezed them a little too much at the sleepover. It's a good thing you didn't see them before Nelia fixed them. They were lopsided."

"Why didn't you tell me?"

"There wasn't anything to tell. Nelia says they'll grow back."

Mom nodded. "Let's hope they grow back soon," she said sharply.

When Nelia returned to our table, Mom said, "That must have been some sleepover."

"Mom doesn't like my eyebrows," I said.

"It is a change," Nelia said.

"Did you know Loren was going to reshape her eyebrows, Nelia?" Mom asked.

Nelia's eyebrows did a high jump. "Mom," I said. "It's not Nelia's fault. She didn't know. I didn't know. It just happened."

"I can see that," Mom said, as the waitress put our plates in front of us. For a while nobody said anything but "Please pass the ketchup." Then Nelia asked Mom about the exhibit.

It was a good question, because Mom forgot about my eyebrows. "I always feel very special when people come to the gallery and tell me how touched they are by my painting," she said.

96

"Everyone wants to know who my model is. And I tell them, *my daughter.*"

I didn't say anything. It made me feel kind of weird inside that people I don't know are looking at Mom's painting and asking questions about me.

"So, daughter, tell me what you have been doing besides getting your eyebrows plucked," Mom said. She was smiling, so I knew she wasn't too mad.

"I'm working on my family-tree project," I said. "Nelia told me lots of stuff about her grandparents. They eloped."

"They did? I didn't know you had a romantic history, Nelia," Mom said.

Nelia nodded. "We have that in common, Mari," she said. "Your family has a romantic history, too."

"Mom, what's romantic about you? Did your grandparents elope?"

Mom laughed. "No. Margery, my grandmother, was not the eloping kind. She didn't approve of running off and getting married but . . ." Mom smiled at me. "Rimini and my mother did. They eloped."

"Hey," I said, "I have romance on both sides of the family." Nelia and Mom laughed. I hoped that meant they weren't going to fight anymore.

On the way home, I asked Mom why she didn't talk much about being a kid. "I told you the important things, Loren. My mother died when I was a baby. Rimini thought my grandmother could take better care of me, so I lived with her in New York. And," Mom turned around and smiled at me, "I went to the Claremont Academy."

"But, Mom," I interrupted, "I know all that. I want to know the romantic stuff about your mom and Rimini."

Mom shook her head. "There's nothing more to tell, Loren," she said.

As we pulled in the driveway, I remembered Mom hadn't told me why she went to New York. When I asked her about it, she said, "Loren, I'm too tired to talk about New York now. We'll talk about it tomorrow. Tell me more about school."

"I'm glad you can come to the swimming meet tomorrow," I said. "I want you to meet Ms. Lyndstrom, my coach. She's really neat."

The next morning, Ellie rode with Mom, Nelia,

and me to the meet. We had to be there an hour early for warm-up and the team meeting. Janelle and Kaitlin met us at our lockers.

Ellie pulled my ponytail tight and tucked all my hair into my cap. When we were ready, we headed for the pool. At the count of three, the four of us jumped into the water. We practiced our strokes, starts, and turns.

When Ms. Lyndstrom blew her whistle, we finished up our laps sprints. "My heart is racing," I said, as we climbed out.

"For RJ?" Ellie teased, as she came up behind me. I pushed her back into the pool.

"Dolphins, over here!" Ms. Lyndstrom shouted. As we hurried to the far end of the pool, I looked for Mom and Nelia. I spotted them in the third row of the bleachers. They didn't see me because they were too busy talking.

"Listen up," Ms. Lyndstrom said when we reached her. "You and the Racers are evenly matched, so it's going to be close. What does that tell you about scoring?"

We all raised our hands. Ms. Lyndstrom called on me. "It means every event is important for the team score."

Ms. Lyndstrom nodded. "You've got it, Loren,"

she said. "Okay. Now, all you Dolphins, remember what?"

"We're a team!"

Ms. Lyndstrom nodded. "That's right. I know you can go the distance. Your muscles will remember what you've learned in workouts. And," Ms. Lyndstrom paused, "what do you do if you get a cramp?"

We answered, "Keep going and swim the cramp out."

"Good, we're ready. Go, Dolphins, go!" Ms. Lyndstrom chanted.

"Go Dolphins. Go! Go! Go!" we responded.

Ellie and I stood behind the block waiting for our event. "Pray no one throws up this time," Ellie whispered as we swung our arms back and forth.

"Swimmers, take your mark!" Ellie and I jumped into the water for the backstroke race. I crouched and held on to the block. When the gun went off, I pushed off with my legs and started my flutter kick. I was moving through the water full speed ahead until I ran into the lane rope. I finished third.

After all the events were over, when we were

drying our hair in the locker room, Ms. Lyndstrom came around and talked to us.

"Good job, Loren," she said to me. "You're a fine strong swimmer."

"Thanks," I said. Ms. Lyndstrom has a way of making you feel good about yourself. "I didn't think I'd make it during freestyle," I told her. "I was sure my cap was going to split, just like last time."

Ms. Lyndstrom nodded. "Hair as long as yours can be a problem for swimmers," she said. "Did you ever think about getting it cut?"

"All the time," I answered.

When we met Mom and Nelia at the car, they congratulated Ellie and me. "The Dolphins are quite a team," Nelia said.

Right before we got out of the car, Ellie whispered to me, "I think RJ's going to call you."

"When?" I whispered back.

Ellie shrugged and said, "I don't know for sure."

When we walked into the kitchen, Agatha came running up to me and rubbed against my legs. "Do you think she knows the Dolphins won?" I asked Nelia.

"Absolutely," Nelia said. "Agatha is a very smart cat."

Mom put her arm across my shoulders. "That was an exciting meet, Loren," she said. "I'm proud of you. You did very well."

"Thanks, Mom. I could do even better if I got my hair cut," I blurted out. I told Mom and Nelia what Ms. Lyndstrom had said.

Mom frowned and crossed her arms in front of her chest. "I'm surprised your coach would make a *personal* remark about your hair, Loren."

"She didn't mean anything bad. It's just that my hair is too long."

"That's her opinion," Mom said sharply.

"It's my opinion, too, Mom. My cap split at the last meet and I thought for sure it would today."

Mom's earrings jangled as she shook her head. "I can't believe you want to cut your beautiful hair for . . . swimming."

"It's not just for swimming. It's for the team . . . and for me." I practically whispered *me*.

"You won't always be on a team," Mom said.

"Yes I will, until I'm out of college."

"Mari, Loren," Nelia said, interrupting our fight, "I have to revise my chapter. I'll be upstairs."

"Nelia, wait," I said. "Tell Mom how much I want to get my hair cut."

"I . . ." Nelia hesitated, "I think your mother already knows that, Loren."

"Loren, I wish you hadn't said that to Nelia," Mom said softly after Nelia left the kitchen.

I lowered my voice, too. "Why? She knows. I told her."

"I suppose she does." Then Mom surprised me and said, "Let's go to the garden room, and talk this over. I don't want to spend our time quarreling."

Just as we sat down, the phone rang. It was Ellie. "RJ chickened out. He asked me to call you."

"About what?" I asked.

"RJ, Nolan, and I are going to ride up to Marvel's and then go to McDonald's. RJ really wants you to come. Can you?"

"I don't think so."

"Ask."

I looked over at Mom. If I asked her, Mom might say I could go, but if I left, I knew she'd be either mad or sad, or both.

"I can't go. Tell RJ about my mom being here and call me later."

When I went back to the table, Mom said, "Did you forget the painting I'm working on?"

"I thought you were finished with it."

"How could I be finished?"

"Is that why you won't let me get my hair cut, because you want to paint it?"

Mom shook her head. "Your hair is part of who you are, Loren."

"I'd be me with short hair."

"We'll compromise, Loren. When Dad, Rimini, and I come back in December, we'll get your hair trimmed. Okay?"

I shrugged and said, "Okay," but I didn't mean it. Getting my hair trimmed isn't a compromise. Mom always trims my ends.

Later on, while Mom was brushing my hair, I promised myself that some way, I wasn't sure how, I was going to get my hair cut before the next meet.

.chapter twelve.

Swimming always makes me hungry. Even though I ate a ton of pizza at lunch, by four o'clock my stomach was rumbling and roaring. Mom, Nelia, and I were going out for dinner, Nelia's treat this time. But we weren't going until six o'clock, so I had to eat something.

While I was spreading peanut butter on some melba rounds, I overheard Mom and Nelia talking. The garden room is right off the kitchen, so it wasn't as if I were eavesdroping or anything. "I'm going to tell her," I heard Mom say.

The *her* had to be me, so I tiptoed closer to the door and listened. "When?" Nelia asked. "Right before you leave?"

"Nelia," Mom said. Her voice was high and sharp. "I don't understand why you think Loren is going to be so upset. I know my own daughter."

"Mari," Nelia said. Her voice was just as sharp as Mom's. "You can't just spring news like that on Loren."

"News? What news?" I asked as I walked into the room. Maybe Mom's going to have a baby, I thought.

Nelia picked up Agatha and said, "Agatha and I have a few things to do before dinner, so I'll leave you two to talk."

"Mom, are you going to have a baby?" I asked as soon as Nelia left the room.

"A baby? Whatever gave you an idea like that, Loren?"

I shrugged. "I couldn't think of any other news."

Mom smiled. "Well, I do have some news, but it's not about a baby."

I sat down on the floor, looked up at Mom, and waited.

Mom joined me on the floor. "Do you remember that day on the beach when your dad and I told you you were going to *visit* Nelia?"

"Yeah. I remember." I grinned at Mom. "I did the

brat routine. Now I'm glad we're here. But what's the news, Mom? Why did you go to New York?"

"I went to our apartment."

"Why? People are living there."

Mom shook her head. "They moved out last month, so my news is, we're moving back in January. And, here's the best part, Rimini is going to stay with us while he illustrates the fairy tales."

"*No!*" The word exploded in my mouth. "We're not . . . moving. I'm not moving. I just got here. I'm on the swimming team. I'm not leaving Lake Shore."

"Loren, your dad and I *know* how hard it is for you to change schools. After we move back to New York, you'll never have to change schools again. You've been accepted at Claremont Academy."

"The boarding school. You want to lock me up in a boarding school."

"Loren, I've made arrangements with Madame Picard; you'll only have to stay at Claremont when your dad and I are traveling, which won't be very often. You won't have to leave the school until it's time for college."

I stood up. "I'm not going. And you can't make me."

"Loren," Mom pressed her fingers against her

head. "I can't believe you're acting like this. I thought you'd be excited."

"Well, you thought wrong! I'm calling Dad."

"He's not there."

"It's eleven o'clock in Italy. Why isn't he at home?"

"He's probably at one of the cafes with Rimini. Loren." Mom stood up and moved closer to me.

I moved back. "I'm calling Dad," I said. "I'll keep on calling until he gets home."

"Fine," Mom said. "Maybe you'll listen to him. Maybe he can do a better job of explaining it."

Mom was wrong on both accounts. When Dad finally answered the phone, he couldn't explain any better than Mom why we had to leave Lake Shore. He gave me the same old arguments Mom did. "Loren," Dad said, "I'm sorry you got the impression we were going to stay with Nelia. We said a *visit*."

"I thought I'd . . . we'd be here at least for junior high. I have friends here. I'm on the swimming team. I don't want to be the new kid again, Dad."

"Loren, I know this is difficult for you now, but when you get to Claremont, you'll make new friends."

"How do you know? I'm not going!" I shouted. "I'm staying here with Nelia." And then I banged down the phone as hard as I could.

When the phone rang again, I knew it was Dad calling back. Mom picked it up right away.

There was no place to go but my room. The tenth stair creaked as usual. Nelia must have heard me because she called out to me. I didn't answer her. All along, the whole time, Nelia knew about Claremont and she didn't tell me.

I slammed my bedroom door as hard as I could. I'm not going to cry, I told myself as I stood in front of my dollhouse. It's funny how tears can spill out of your eyes and splash down on your shirt before you even know you're crying.

When I heard the knock on the door, I didn't move. "Loren, it's Nelia. May I come in?"

"No." I didn't care if I was rude. I didn't want to talk to *anybody.*

"All right," Nelia said softly. "I'll talk to you later."

I went to the door and opened it. Nelia was walking down the stairs very slowly. "Why didn't you tell me?" I called after her in a half whisper. Nelia came back up the stairs and opened her arms to me, and I ran right into them. "I'm not going," I sniffled.

We didn't go out for dinner. Mom went to bed with a headache, and Nelia and I ate canned chicken noodle soup. "I can stay here, can't I?" I asked Nelia.

Nelia sighed. "You know how much I love having you here with me," she said, "and how much I want you to stay, but . . ."

I shook my head. "I'm staying. No way am I leaving Lake Shore or you."

The next morning, Mom came to my room. She sat down on my bed and said, "I'm sorry you're so upset."

I didn't say anything, I just stared up at the ceiling and pretended I was floating. No one can make you talk if you don't want to, and I didn't want to talk to Mom.

Finally, Mom said, "We have to resolve this, Loren."

I sat up, grabbed my pillow, and held it close to my chest. "I'm not going, Mom. You and dad and Rimini can go to New York, but I'm staying here . . . with Nelia."

Mom got up and walked over to my dollhouse. She straightened a picture and moved the sofa and chairs around the living room. "Did Nelia say you could stay here?" she asked.

I didn't answer Mom. She turned around and said, "Sometimes you have to do things just because you have to do them. This is one of those times, Loren."

Before I knew it happened, I threw my pillow at Mom. She picked it up and put it back on my bed without saying anything.

Mom and I just stared at each other for one very long minute. Then Mom said, "We'll talk about this later, Loren."

I got up and walked over to my dollhouse. Room by room, I packed up the furniture, lamps, rugs, the piano, the easel, the palette, and all the little pieces that I had arranged and rearranged. When I was finished, I carried the house and the furniture downstairs. It took three trips.

While I was stacking the boxes in the front closet, Mom came into the foyer. "What are you doing, Loren?"

"I packed up the dollhouse. You can bring it to New York. I won't need it here."

Mom tugged on her earring and sighed. "Why are you acting this way?"

"Why are we moving?"

111

"For many reasons, but most of all because it's time to go home. And New York is our home. And Rimini is going to be with us."

"Why is that such a big deal?"

Mom sighed again. "I want you to know him. I thought you'd be very excited to model for him."

"I hate being a model."

"Oh, Loren." Mom gave a half-laugh and shook her head. "You don't mean that."

"Why do you always say that when I tell you how I feel? Why won't you listen to me? I don't want to go to New York. I don't want to model for Rimini. And I don't want to go to Claremont Academy."

"Loren." Mom frowned. "I thought you'd be happy to know that you won't change schools again."

"It's not just changing school." Somehow I had to make Mom understand. "It's changing my whole life."

"Changes can be very good for us, Loren."

"I don't want to change anymore. I want to stay in one place."

"That's what this is all about," Mom said. "You won't have to leave Claremont."

"I don't want to leave Lake Shore."

112

Mom shook her head. "I just don't understand you. When we lived in New York, you told me you couldn't wait until you were old enough to go to Claremont. Now you're old enough and you don't want to go."

"Right! I want to stay here, but you want to pack me up like a piece of dollhouse furniture and plop me any old place." I opened the front door and ran across the lawn to Ellie and RJ's house.

Mom called after me to come back, but I just kept on going.

·chapter thirteen·

RJ was shooting hoops in his driveway. "Where's Ellie?" I asked.

"She's at the dentist with my mom," RJ said.

I leaned against the tree and watched RJ dribble the ball. "Want to play?" he asked.

"Okay."

RJ passed me the ball. I kept missing the basket.

"What's wrong with *you*?" RJ asked.

"Everything."

"Huhh? What do you mean?"

"I'm moving."

"You just moved *here*."

I shrugged. "It doesn't make any difference."

RJ slam dunked the ball and then he asked me if I wanted a soda. I said I didn't care.

When he came out of the house with two cans of root beer, we sat on the stairs. At first, RJ didn't say anything and neither did I, we just drank our sodas. Finally RJ asked, "When are you going?"

"We're supposed to be in New York right after Christmas. But I'm trying to figure out how to stay here."

"Any luck?" RJ asked.

I sucked on a piece of my hair and said, "Don't I wish. I just keep on saying I'm *not* going."

"It doesn't work," RJ said. "Ellie and I tried that when we lived in Washington."

"Thanks a lot. I don't know what else to do."

RJ squeezed his pop can, and then handed it to me. "What you need is the Shape Changer."

I rolled my eyes at RJ. "Yeah, right. Maybe he could turn me into a real dolphin and I could just swim away."

"Have you got a better idea?" RJ asked, as his mother pulled the car into the driveway.

"What are you guys doing?" Ellie asked.

"Loren's moving," RJ announced.

"Not if I can *do* something about it," I said.

Before Ellie could say anything, Mom was there

standing on RJ and Ellie's driveway. "Loren, we have to leave for the airport in ten minutes."

"See you guys," I said.

Mom and I walked back to the house. I didn't talk to her and she didn't talk to me. I headed for the bathroom. When I came out, Mom was waiting in the hall for me. "Where's Nelia?" I asked.

"She's upstairs. She'll be down in a minute," Mom replied.

I turned and headed for the kitchen. "Loren," Mom called sharply. "Wait."

Mom came up to me and put her arms around me. "I can't leave you like this."

More than anything I wanted to snuggle in close to Mom, but I couldn't. It was as if there were boards tied to my chest and back. I couldn't bend.

Mom put her hands on my cheeks. "Your dad and I are choosing what is best for us . . . as a family."

"You get to choose. Why can't I?"

"Loren, you have to come with us."

"Why? You left me with Nelia once before. Why won't you let me stay here now?"

Mom didn't answer me right away. She

breathed in and out, then she said, "This time it's different."

"Why? What's different about it?"

"We went to Europe without you because Rimini . . . your grandfather was very sick. I didn't have a choice. Now I do."

"But I don't have a choice, about anything," I muttered.

"If you want to put it that way, you're right, Loren," Mom said. "We're your parents and you don't have a choice."

Nobody said anything on the way to the airport. When we pulled up to the curb at Air Italia, Mom opened the car door, turned around and said, "Thanks, Nelia."

"Safe journey, Mari," Nelia said. "We'll see you in December."

I got out of the car. Mom put down her bag and hugged me. This time I hugged her back. "I'll talk to you soon, Loren," Mom said. "And I'll see you on your birthday."

I nodded, opened the car door, and climbed in next to Nelia. On the way home, Nelia said, "One dollar for your thoughts."

"How come nobody listens to kids?"

Nelia smiled at me. "I don't know about kids," she said, "but I'll listen to you."

"I don't have any choices. I'm here and then *poof* I'm not here."

"Your mother told me you wouldn't have to leave Claremont."

"I don't want to go *there*. It's a stuck-up school and they probably don't even have a swimming team. And the worst part is I know Mom, Dad, and Rimini will be halfway around the world most of the time and I'll be there all by myself."

"You don't know that for sure, Loren."

"Yes, I do. Mom likes the sun. I bet you six million dollars when it snows in New York, they'll go where it's warm."

Nelia sighed. "I doubt that, Loren. I think they're settling down."

"Maybe you do, but I don't."

"I wish there was something I could do to help you."

"Why can't you?"

"I can't because the problem is between your mom and your dad, and you. You wouldn't want me to be the nosy old grandmother butting her nose into your family business."

"Is that why you didn't tell me about Claremont and everything?" Nelia nodded. After that, we didn't talk much. We just listened to the radio. Nelia let me play B96.

When we got home, I asked Nelia if I could call Stephanie. She said yes.

As soon as Stephanie answered the phone, I told her I was moving.

"You are?" she shrieked. "Back here to Los Olas?"

"That would be good news. We're moving to New York."

"That's as far as Chicago."

"Tell me about it. And tell me what I'm going to *do* about it."

"Why don't you stay with your grandmother?"

"*They* won't let me. And Nelia says there's nothing she can do about it."

"Ask your grandfather? Maybe he can help."

"Rimini. He doesn't know me. And besides he's in Italy."

"So call him up. You're always calling your mom."

"Steph, maybe that's it! Maybe Rimini can talk to Mom for me. It's worth a try anyway."

As soon as Stephanie hung up, I called Italy. Finally after a million tries, the phone started ringing. I decided I'd hang up if Dad answered. A deep gruff voice said, "Pronto."

I almost hung up, but I didn't. I took a deep breath and asked, "Is this Rimini?" When he said yes, I said, "This is Loren, your granddaughter in America."

"My little Loren, how are you?'

"I'm okay," I said. But then I didn't know what else to say. It would have been easier to swim in a whirlpool than talk to Rimini about moving or not moving. You can't ask a stranger to help you with a problem, not when it's something personal.

Rimini started talking to me. He told me he was sketching castles, cottages, and spinning wheels, teaching Dad to make pasta, and painting in the morning light with Mom. "I hope you had a most happy time with your mother, Loren. She misses you every day, as your father and I do."

"How can you miss me?" I blurted out. "You don't know me."

"This is so very true. I have planned for such a very long time to come and see you, to get to know you . . . but life . . . my work . . . I would get into a painting and I couldn't get out of it."

"It's okay," I said.

"But soon we will be together. And I will get to know my little Loren."

Boy, some nerve, I thought. *I'm not your little Loren* I wanted to shout, but before I could say anything, Rimini said very softly, "I'm glad you called me."

"I called to tell you . . . Mom's plane left on time."

"Good. Good. Your father is on his way to the airport to meet her. It is long drive, so he is taking plenty of time."

"Well, I have to go now. Good-bye."

"Good-bye for now. I will see you soon. And I will tell your mother and father you called."

"You don't have to do that."

"Oh, but I must. They will want to know."

Great. Just great. No way, not in a hundred years is Mom ever going to believe I called to tell Rimini her plane left on time.

.chapter fourteen.

Mom called early the next morning. She didn't say anything about my calling Rimini. She didn't say anything about anything. We talked about her flight, and she said she missed me and would call soon. "If you need me, call me anytime," Mom said.

I hope someday someone writes a book on how to understand parents, especially when they pretend everything is all right and it isn't. Dad got on the speaker phone with Mom. All he said was that he was counting the days until my birthday. Both Mom and Dad said in sync, "Love you. See you soon."

School and swimming practice kept me busy.

Nelia let me call Stephanie once a week. When I told her I wimped out with Rimini, she shrieked, "You can't go there! You're supposed to move back here."

It's weird how time can change your mind. When I came to Lake Shore in September, I wanted to go back to Los Olas. Now it was October and I wanted to stay here, but I didn't tell that to Stephanie.

Mom and Dad called twice a week. They told me that Mom had just about finished painting *Loren by the Sea*, that they would be in England for a week and in Paris for two weeks, but they never said one word about New York or Claremont. A tiny little seed of hope began to grow that maybe, maybe they changed their minds. Maybe they believed me when I said I wouldn't go.

Two days before Halloween, when Mom and Dad called, I almost asked them if they'd changed their minds, but at the last minute, I chickened out. Instead I told them about Lake Shore's fall festival.

RJ, Nolan, Ellie, and I dressed up for the festival. RJ dressed as Spider-Man, Nolan was Dick Tracy, I was Dorothy, and Ellie was the Wizard of Oz.

At the longest hair contest, they measured my

braids and I won. RJ and Nolan took off with half my prize, the world's longest stick of bubble gum.

Right after Halloween, we started practicing extra hours for the champion meet. "I wish it wasn't the Saturday after Thanksgiving," Kaitlin said. "I'll still be stuffed with turkey."

"A stuffed stomach isn't as bad as a bathing cap stuffed with hair," I said.

At the next practice, it happened again—my bathing cap split open. "What am I going to do?" I asked Ellie on our way home. "If we lose the meet because of my hair . . ." I couldn't even finish the sentence.

Ellie said, "Chill out, Loren, that won't happen."

"I wish, I wish, I wish I could get my hair cut," I muttered.

"I've got an idea," Ellie said. "Why don't you have Ms. Lyndstrom write a letter to your Mom? Maybe she could convince her to let you cut your hair."

"I already tried that. Mom got mad at Ms. Lyndstrom."

When I walked into the house, Nelia and Agatha were waiting for me in the kitchen. "What's up?" I asked.

"A letter came for you today," Nelia said.

"From Mom and Dad?" Nelia shook her head. "From Stephanie?" Nelia shook her head again. "I give up—wait . . . Rimini?"

"No, it's from"—Nelia rubbed her forehead with her finger—"it's from the academy."

"Claremont?" I squeaked. Nelia handed me the letter. It was from Madame Picard.

It didn't take me long to read it. "Madame says I am very welcome," I told Nelia. "And she's proud Mom is sending me there, to carry on the Claremont tradition." My voice cracked when I said, "She wants my measurements so my uniforms will be ready in January."

I threw the letter on the table and slumped down into the chair across from Nelia.

People say when you drown, your past life flashes before you. I felt like I was drowning, but I was seeing the future. For the next six years, I'd be wearing a dorky uniform, spending every day with strangers, and always being odd one out.

Agatha jumped out of Nelia's lap and onto mine. I stroked her back, letting my fingers feel her long white hair.

"What am I going to do, Nelia? It's not fair." Nelia started to answer me, but I just went right on talking. "Mom and Dad never ask me what I want to do. Where does it say kids aren't supposed to have choices?"

Nelia's dark blue eyes glistened. "You don't have a choice about school, but you do have other choices, Loren."

"Like what?'

"Well," Nelia gave a little smile, "it's not easy to do, but you can choose your attitude toward and about things."

I hunched up my shoulders and thought, Yeah right, I can do that. I can have an attitude.

Nelia stood up. "How about going in the basement and throwing a few pots? I always feel better when I get my hands in clay."

I shook my head. "Maybe later," I said.

After Nelia left, I picked up the letter from Madame Picard, pushed Agatha off my lap, and went out to the garage for my bike. I didn't care if it was raining, I just wanted to get to the lake.

I stood on the pier for a long time, listening to the whitecaps race to the shore. Lake Michigan isn't the ocean, but it was the closest thing I had to it. When I stopped crying, I took the letter from Madame Picard out of my pocket and tore it into tiny pieces. I watched the whitecaps swallow them.

"Hey, Monroe!" RJ rode up to me. "What are you, goofy? It's pouring rain."

"So tell me something I don't know," I snapped at RJ.

RJ grinned. "Race you home," he said.

Fallen leaves made the streets too slippery to race, so we rode side by side. "Your grandmother's looking for you," RJ said.

"How do you know?"

"She came over to my house."

"Oh."

"I told her I knew where you were. When I was riding back from Marvel's, I saw you heading toward the lake."

"And you came out in the rain again . . . because of me? Why?"

RJ shrugged and said, "Only the Shape Changer knows."

Only RJ can make you laugh while rain is pouring down on your head. When I turned into my driveway, I said, "Thanks, RJ."

He said, "See ya."

Nelia was waiting for me in the kitchen. All she said was, "Take a hot shower and then we'll talk."

When I came back downstairs, Nelia was sitting in the garden room watching the rain. She made room for me on the sofa. Agatha and I curled up next to her. "Things have a way of working out, Loren," Nelia said.

I didn't say anything. I just put my head on her shoulder.

It rained most of November. RJ, Ellie, Nolan, and I went to the movies twice. Ellie talked me into wearing strawberry lip gloss, just in case. We all sat together, but nobody kissed anybody. I finished my family-tree project. And I swam in the morning and I swam after school. We practiced the dolphin kick, concentrated on streamlining, and turned somersaults in the water every chance we got.

At our last practice, which was the day before Thanksgiving, my cap split open again. I came up out of the water looking like the monster from the deep.

"We're not going to win, because of *me*," I said to Ms. Lyndstrom.

"Loren, you're going to do just fine. You're ready for the meet, and whatever happens, the Dolphins are true champions."

In the locker room, I said to Ellie, "I don't care what Mom says, I'm going to cut my hair."

Ellie put her hand on my forehead. "Are you

sick in the head? You know if you cut it, it won't grow back by the time your parents come home. And you'll be in major, major trouble. Your mom's painting you . . . with long hair."

"It's my hair."

"Yeah, but what if she grounds you until it grows back?"

"What am I going to do, Ellie? I don't want the Dolphins to lose because of me."

"Braid your hair as tight as you can and pray they don't pop out of your cap."

"What if they do?"

"Just swim," Ellie said.

Easy for you to say, I thought. Ellie's hair is shorter than RJ's.

I woke up on Thanksgiving morning with a stomachache. It got worse when I was talking to Mom, but it disappeared when Nelia and I went next door for dinner.

Nelia and I had planned to go by ourselves to a fancy hotel for dinner, but when RJ and Ellie's parents invited us to share their turkey, Nelia and I said yes. On the way home, Nelia and I agreed being part of a family dinner was more fun than a hotel.

The next morning, cramps in my stomach woke

me up. Great. Just great, I thought. I can't be sick!

I wasn't. I had it! I had my period and the meet was tomorrow.

Nelia was still asleep, so I called Ellie. The night of her sleepover, when we had told each other our secrets, I had confessed that I was probably the only one on the team that didn't have their period. "Can you believe it? Why did it have to come now?" I moaned to Ellie.

"I got mine last year. In school."

"I know, but you didn't have to swim."

"That's no big deal," Ellie said.

When I told Nelia, she frowned and said, "I don't know if you should swim in a meet."

"It's okay, Nelia. Everybody does it. I know what to do."

Nelia's eyes filled with tears. She said, "You're growing up so quickly, Loren."

I shrugged and said, "I wondered if I'd ever get it."

Nelia smiled. "You'd better call your mother and tell her."

"No! Mom might say I can't swim in the meet. Please don't make me call her. I'll tell her when she comes home."

Nelia sighed. "I don't know, Loren."

"Please. If Mom says I can't do it, I'll let the Dolphins down."

Nelia raised her eyebrows. Then she said, "It's your choice, Loren." I gave her a big hug.

Saturday morning, while I was braiding my hair, a tiny cramp hit me. I took a deep breath and it went away. What if I get one in the middle of the relay race? What if my cap bursts open at the same time?

"I'm really going to be a drag on the team," I said to my reflection in the mirror.

I pulled my braids so tight my head hurt. It's not going to work, I thought. You can't swim with a headache.

There was only one thing to do.

·chapter fifteen·

I pulled all the pictures Stephanie sent me out of the drawer. "What do you think, Steph?" I asked her picture. "Should I cut off my braids at my ears or at my shoulders?"

No answer. I closed my eyes and snipped off my hair, at my ears. Two sand-colored braids fell to the floor. I picked them up and threw them into my bottom dresser drawer.

I was a free bird. No more hair to drag me down. I grabbed the Cubs cap Ellie had given me, plopped it on my head, and ran out of my room. I didn't look in the mirror.

I whizzed by Nelia, who was polishing her blue

bowl at the kitchen table. "See you at the meet. Ellie's waiting for me."

When I got in the car, Ellie asked, "Why are you wearing your baseball cap?"

I took it off. Ellie shrieked, *"Yeeee . . . You . . . Holy! . . . Ohhhhh. My . . ."*

She was so loud, Mrs. Blake turned around. "Ellie, what's—Loren, your hair! What happened to your hair?"

"I cut it."

"You butchered—" Ellie stopped. "I don't be-lieve it," she said.

I hunched up my shoulders. "Now I won't have to worry about my swimming cap."

Janelle and Kaitlin almost fell into the pool when they saw me. "It looks good," Kaitlin said. Ms. Lyndstrom didn't say anything.

Kaitlin, Janelle, Ellie, and I were the four legs in the relay race. We were neck and neck, until one of the Racers turned into a speed demon at the end of the last lap.

"We didn't win," I moaned in the locker room.

"Hey, that's okay," Ms. Lyndstrom said. "Don't knock second place. You guys swam your hearts out. And that's what counts." Ms. Lyndstrom put her hand on my shoulder. "And who knows," she said, "next meet, with a lot more hard work and lots of practice, we might outrace the Racers."

Not me, I thought. I'll be trying to stand on my toes in a dumb ballet class or something. I raced for the toilet. Everybody heard me throw up.

When I came out, Crystal poked Patty, but nobody said anything. Ellie handed me her dryer. It took about two minutes to dry my hair. I plopped my Cubs cap back on my head and wondered if I'd have to wear it for the next ten years.

Nelia was waiting for me in her car. "Good job," she said. I shrugged. Nelia looked at me and frowned. "You're so pale, Loren. Don't you feel well?"

I reached up and took off my cap. "Oh my! Oh, my God!" Nelia screamed. "Your hair. It's gone!'

"I wanted the Dolphins to win."

For a minute, Nelia didn't say anything. Then I heard her say softly to herself, "What's done is done."

"Mom's going to kill me."

Nelia glanced over at me. "We'll worry about your mom later. Right now, we have to get you to my beauty salon."

Patrice, the woman who cuts Nelia's hair,

washed, combed, and brushed my hair. "We will do bangs," she said, after she turned my head from side to side. "And then you will have the perfect gamine look."

"What's the gamine look?" I asked.

"The look, very short and very sassy. It is almost, but not quite, what you have now," Patrice replied. "I will shape your hair to your head."

When she was finished, Patrice handed me a mirror. "I don't look like me," I said.

"Ah," Patrice said, and she shook her head, "with your small face and those lovely, lovely dark eyes"—she smiled and nodded—"you will *soon* know it is you."

As we were driving home, Nelia said, "Loren, you know you have to call your parents and tell them."

I pretended I didn't hear what Nelia said, I just leaned my head back on the seat and closed my eyes.

Nelia flipped on the radio. It was tuned to the jazz station she likes. The music was soft and sad. I didn't ask if I could switch stations.

When we walked into the kitchen, Agatha ran right up to me. "Agatha knows me," I said.

"Of course she does," Nelia said. "Why wouldn't she? A haircut doesn't change who you are."

Nelia and I sat at the table. She sipped her hot tea, and I stared at my glass of ginger ale. "Loren, your parents have to *know* before they walk in the door."

I shook my head. I didn't want to think or talk about Mom or Dad.

Nelia wouldn't let go of it. "Don't you think seeing you with short hair would be more than a big surprise?"

"They're always surprising me. Why can't I surprise them?"

"Loren, we're not going to argue about this, I'll call them if you want or you can tell them." Nelia reached out for my hand. "It's your choice."

I pulled my hand away. "That's not a choice," I said. "I don't have any choices."

"You chose to cut your hair."

"Why are you taking their side?"

Nelia pushed her chair back. "This isn't about sides, Loren. Your parents must be told before they walk in the door."

"Why? Cutting your hair isn't a crime." I put my hands on the back of my head. Something was missing, a part of me was gone. I flew out of the kitchen and up the stairs.

Nelia found me in my bedroom, rocking back and forth on the floor, holding my braids close to my ears. She sat down on the floor with me and held me close for a long time.

The next morning, I called Mom. I tried to tell her, but nothing came out of my mouth. Finally, I managed to say, "I look different."

"What do you mean different?" Mom's voice rose. "Are you all right? Did you hurt yourself again?"

"No. I . . . my hair . . ." I looked over at Nelia.

"You can do it. Tell her," Nelia whispered.

I took one giant breath and said as fast as I could, "I cut my hair."

"You did what?" Mom shrieked.

I handed the phone to Nelia. Every part of me wanted to run upstairs and hide, but I stayed and listened to Nelia tell Mom about the swimming meet, my period, calling Rimini, the letter from Claremont, and Patrice.

When I got back on the phone again, Mom's voice was very low. "Why didn't you tell me about your period?" she asked.

"Huh?" I thought for sure Mom would yell and

scream about my haircut. "I didn't say anything because I thought you might not let me swim in the meet."

If Mom's sigh rippled across the ocean, there would have been a giant tidal wave. "We'll be home Friday, Loren," she said. "We'll talk then."

Monday morning, Ellie, RJ, and Nolan were waiting for me in the driveway. "At least you didn't get a buzz," RJ said. Ellie whacked him with her notebook.

When we were locking our bikes in the rack, RJ said, "You know, Monroe, you don't look all that bad in short hair."

I touched my naked neck. "Thanks."

When I came home from school on Friday, the day Mom, Dad, and Rimini were coming back, the kitchen smelled like onions and garlic. This was very weird, because on Fridays we order out. Nelia was sitting on the table chopping away. "What are you doing?" I asked.

"I'm making spaghetti sauce," Nelia replied.

"Why are you doing that? You always just open a jar."

Nelia whacked another onion. "I can't write, I've dusted and vacuumed the whole house twice, so I thought I'd cook dinner for your parents and Rimini."

When Nelia fusses, she's worried about something. And I knew what it was. "You think Mom and Dad are going to be mad at *you* because of me, don't you?"

Nelia shook her head. "That's not true, Loren."

"Yes it is. You think there's *no* chance at all that they'll let me stay here with you, because of what I did."

"I don't think there ever was a chance," Nelia said. "Did you?" I shook my head.

Nelia and I heard the car door close. "Let's go," Nelia said.

I looked for my Cubs hat, but I couldn't find it. When Nelia opened the front door, Mom, Dad, and a thin short man were standing on the porch. I tried not to stare at his black eye patch and lion-headed cane.

Mom didn't scream when she saw me. All she did was kiss and hug me. Dad gave me a tight hug, too, and said, "Boy, have I missed you."

Rimini kissed me on both cheeks and held out his arms. "I have waited so long to see you, my little Loren."

Everyone was polite. I kept waiting, but no one said anything about my hair. Rimini told Nelia her spaghetti sauce was worthy of a true Italian. And Mom and Rimini did the dishes, while Nelia and I listened to Dad play the piano.

When I couldn't hide my yawns any longer, I gave everybody, even Rimini, a quick kiss. Then I ran up the stairs to my room and shut the door.

I had just closed my eyes when my door opened. It was Mom. She sat on the edge of my bed for a while without saying anything. Then she brushed my bangs off my face and said, "It will take me a little while to get used to the gamine look. Did you . . . did you save your hair?"

I jumped up, opened my drawer, and handed Mom my braids. "You can have them," I said.

Mom shook her head. "They belong to you, Loren. Why would you want to give them to me?"

"Because . . . you know . . . my . . . my hair belonged to you, sort of, more than it did to me."

Mom gave me a look I couldn't read. It probably meant she was mad about what I said. After she walked over to my dresser and put my braids back in the drawer, she said, "You must be tired. I know I am. Why don't you get back into bed."

When I pulled my comforter up to my chin, Mom leaned over and kissed my forehead. "We'll talk tomorrow."

Yeah. Right. Sure, I thought. The way Mom said *talk*, I knew she meant *I'll talk, you listen.*

As Mom headed for the door, it hit me. *Tomorrow! Tomorrow is my birthday!* Getting yelled at on your birthday isn't something to look forward to, so I threw back my comforter and sat up. "Why don't you yell at me now?"

No answer. Mom closed my door behind her. I guess she didn't hear me.

·chapter sixteen·

Twelve balloons, one more than last year, were floating around my door when I woke up. And a "Happy Birthday" sign was hung along the railing.

Mom and Dad were still sleeping, so I went downstairs. Rimini was in the kitchen. So was Nelia. Both of them sang "Happy Birthday" when they saw me.

Nelia gave me a birthday kiss and said, "I'm going to take my shower now."

Nelia was leaving me with *Rimini.* Why?

"A fine woman, your grandmother," Rimini said.

I didn't say anything. Rimini rubbed his hands

together. "What would you like for a birthday breakfast?"

"Cornflakes, I guess."

Rimini looked as if I had said a swear word. "You want to eat those dried-up little chips that you put in a bowl of cold milk?" he asked.

"Yeah. I like them."

"Do you like pizza?" he asked. When I said yes, he said, "Good, I will make egg pizza for your birthday breakfast."

Egg pizza! "You've got to be kidding."

"No. No. It is so . . . so good. You will"—Rimini kissed his fingertips—"love it."

What I'll probably do is barf it up, I thought. "I never heard of egg pizza," I said.

"I will show you," Rimini said. "We will cook together and talk a bit." He opened the refrigerator and rummaged around. Out came eggs, onions, the leftover spaghetti sauce, and a can of Parmesan cheese. He put them on the counter and frowned. "No peppers, no cheese in one piece?" he asked.

I shook my head. "Nelia opens cans."

Rimini laughed. "I will teach her to cook."

While Rimini chopped the onion, I broke the eggs into a bowl. An egg dropped out of my hand

and splattered on the floor, when Rimini said, "Your haircut is most becoming."

I ran to the counter and grabbed a paper towel. While I was wiping up the gloppy mess, I said without thinking, "Aren't you mad at me because I cut off my braids?"

Rimini stopped chopping. "Why would I be angry?" he asked. "It is *your* hair."

"I know, but now I can't be Rapunzel."

"Who says this? You can be whoever you want."

"How? I don't have long hair."

Rimini's eyebrows met in one big frown. "This makes no difference. Do not worry. I, Rimini, have enough imagination to draw long hair."

Great. Just great. Rimini still wants me to be his model. "I've got to go and get dressed," I said.

"No. Sit down, Loren." Rimini patted the chair.

"But . . . I—"

"Sit! Please."

I sat down. Who had a choice?

"We must talk." I didn't know who the *we* was because Rimini did all the talking. "It is like a story, Loren. The first time your mother and father left you to be with me, they came because . . . I was very foolish."

Rimini stopped talking and ran his hand across his beard. He gave a little sigh and said, "I had been driving very fast, so fast the car spun in circles and crashed into a tree."

"Mom told me you were sick."

"She told you the truth. Let me continue my story. Until I could see again"—Rimini touched his black eye patch— "at least out of one eye, your mother became my eyes."

"And"—Rimini thumped his cane on the floor—"your father became my legs."

"What do you mean?" I asked. "I don't get it."

"After the crash, I couldn't see and I couldn't walk. I was Humpty-Dumpty. But your parents put me back together. And Loren—listen to this, this is most important of all—they kept fanning the little spark that gave me hope that once again, I would paint. It took a long time. A year. A year they spent away from you."

"I'm glad you're better."

Rimini laughed and wagged his finger back and forth. "I am better than better, because once more there are Riminis hanging in the galleries of Europe."

"Mom's painting is there, too," I said.

"Yes, I am very proud, as you are." Rimini put

145

his hands under his chin and stared at me. "Do you know, my little Loren, how much your mother and your father miss you . . . whenever you are apart?"

I shrugged and wondered how much longer he was going to talk. Why was he telling me all this?

Rimini continued, "And this last time away from you, oh, how hard it was for them."

Yeah. Right. Now I *knew* why Rimini was telling me all this stuff. He wanted me to stop fighting with Mom and Dad about New York and Claremont.

Before I could say anything, Mom, Dad, and Nelia came into the kitchen singing "Happy Birthday." Fifteen minutes later, we were all sitting down to eat. Rimini presented each of us with a large wedge of the pizza.

Here goes, I thought, as I bit into my piece. It tasted like scrambled eggs, which would be okay—if you like tomato-covered scrambled eggs. I don't. But somehow, I managed to get it all down without barfing or gagging.

After we finished, Mom said, "Loren, why don't you get dressed and we'll ride down to the lake. Nelia said I could borrow her bike."

Mom wore Nelia's winter jacket and her own

white beret. She said she liked the dark green jacket Nelia had bought me. After I put it on, Mom handed me a beret just like hers and said, "I don't want you to catch cold. Wear this."

I almost said, "No way, I'll look like a dork," but I decided Mom would think I was picking a fight, so I plopped the beret on my head and kept my mouth shut.

On our way to the lake, Mom and I were riding into the wind, so we didn't talk much. After we locked our bikes, I ran off down the pier. Mom followed me. The whitecaps were foaming and pounding against the shore. "I miss the ocean, do you?" Mom asked.

I nodded. Mom put her arm across my shoulder, pulled me close, and said, *"Loren by the Sea* will soon be finished."

"But . . . but . . . when you called Wednesday night, you said you'd finished it, that it was all ready to be framed."

Mom gave my shoulder a little squeeze. "I thought it was . . . but—I have a new perspective now."

"You're changing it because of my hair. Why?"

"Loren, I want to paint *you*. Not your hair."

I turned away from Mom and walked back

down the pier. In the sand, at the edge of the pier, I found some skipping stones. The first one I threw out skimmed the surface before it disappeared.

Mom came and stood beside me. "Where did you learn to do that?" she asked.

"RJ taught me."

"Teach me," Mom said.

Mom's fourth stone did a short skim before it disappeared. Each stone we threw skimmed a longer distance. "Go for it," I said as we threw out our last stones. They skipped across the water together before they disappeared.

As we walked back to our bikes, Mom said, "Claremont might not be as bad as you think. I talked to Madame Picard. They do have a swiming team. And some of their swimmers have competed in the Junior Olympics. Who knows, you could be one of them."

Big deal, I thought. I pulled the beret down on my ears and hunched up my shoulders and asked, "When are we leaving?"

"In June."

"June?" My heart did a double somersault. "After school is out? Does that mean I can stay for the rest of the year?"

Mom smiled and nodded. "Yes," she said. "Your dad and I are staying, too."

"Are you kidding?"

"Loren, I wouldn't do that," Mom said softly.

Part of me still didn't believe Mom. It was too good to be true. "How come you and Dad changed your minds?"

"We didn't change our minds. We just changed the time. We're moving to New York in June and I'll tell Madame Picard to expect you next September."

As Mom and I rode back to Nelia's, I thought, At least I can finish the swimming season with the Dolphins. Maybe we'll beat the Racers. And I wouldn't have to say good-bye to Ellie and RJ right away. And by June, I'd really be used to the gamine look. "Does Nelia know?" I asked.

Mom nodded. "Last night, after you went to bed, Rimini, Nelia, your dad, and I had a long talk. We talked about your birthday, how you're growing up, school, moving, all those things."

"Is Rimini staying with us, too?"

"He's going on to New York after Christmas. But he'll be back for visits. He's looking forward to painting in the garden room."

"Can I go back and visit Stephanie?"

"We'll see. Maybe, maybe we can arrange for Stephanie to come to New York."

The rest of the way home, Mom and I didn't talk much, we just rode. As we turned the corner of Nelia's street, Mom said, right out of the blue, "I'm going to help Rimini illustrate the fairy tales. I hope you will pose for us?"

"Do I have a choice?"

"Yes, you do, Loren," Mom said.

"If I can choose . . ." I thought I was going to say *I don't want to do it,* but instead, I surprised myself and asked, "Can I just think about it for a while?" Mom said yes.

When Mom and I opened the back door, we heard Dad playing the piano. Mom and I snuck up behind him and put our cold hands on his neck. He jumped up and chased us around the living room, down the hall, and into the kitchen.

Agatha yowled and raced for the basement. I followed her down the stairs.

Nelia was in the basement showing Rimini the way she throws her pots. "We're staying!" I shouted. "For a little while anyway."

That night, while Dad and Rimini were in the kitchen cooking my birthday dinner, I asked Mom and Nelia if they wanted to help me unpack the dollhouse. I carried the house into Nelia's living room; then Mom, Nelia, and I unpacked the boxes and rearranged the furniture.

By the time Rimini and Dad called us for dinner, Mom, Nelia, and I had the house back together.